Meet Sophie

Also by Nancy Rue

You! A Christian Girl's Guide to Growing Up
Girl Politics
Everyone Tells Me to Be Myself ... but I Don't Know Who I Am

Sophie's World Series
Meet Sophie (Book One)
Sophie Steps Up (Book Two)
Sophie and Friends (Book Three)
Sophie's Friendship Fiasco (Book Four)
Sophie Flakes Out (Book Five)
Sophie's Drama (Book Six)

The Lucy Series
Lucy Doesn't Wear Pink (Book One)
Lucy Out of Bounds (Book Two)
Lucy's Perfect Summer (Book Three)
Lucy Finds Her Way (Book Four)

Other books in the growing Faithgirlz!™ library

Bibles
The Faithgirlz! Bible
NIV Faithgirlz! Backpack Bible

Faithgirlz! Bible Studies
Secret Power of Love
Secret Power of Joy
Secret Power of Goodness
Secret Power of Grace

Fiction

From Sadie's Sketchbook

Shades of Truth (Book One)
Flickering Hope (Book Two)
Waves of Light (Book Three)
Brilliant Hues (Book Four)

The Girls of Harbor View

Girl Power (Book One)
Take Charge (Book Two)
Raising Faith (Book Three)
Secret Admirer (Book Four)

Boarding School Mysteries

Vanished (Book One)
Betrayed (Book Two)
Burned (Book Three)
Poisoned (Book Four)

Nonfiction

Faithgirlz! Handbook
Faithgirlz Journal
Food, Faith, and Fun! Faithgirlz Cookbook
No Boys Allowed
What's a Girl to Do?
Girlz Rock
Chick Chat
Real Girls of the Bible
My Beautiful Daughter
Whatever!

Check out www.faithgirlz.com

faiThGirLz!
the beauty of believing

Meet
Sophie

2 BOOKS IN 1
Includes *Sophie's World*
and *Sophie's Secret*

Nancy Rue

ZONDER**kidz**

ZONDERVAN.com/
AUTHORTRACKER
follow your favorite authors

Dedicated to the original Corn Flake Girls
of Drexel Hill, Pennsylvania:

Brittany, Stephanie M., Lorraine, Jenny, Allison, Sarah,
Julie, Stephanie R., Lauren, Lindsay, and Amanda.

ZONDERKIDZ

www.zonderkidz.com

Meet Sophie
ISBN 978-0310-73850-3

Copyright © 2013 by Nancy Rue

Sophie's World Copyright © 2004 by Nancy Rue
Sophie's Secret Copyright © 2004 by Nancy Rue

This title is also available as a Zondervan ebook.
Visit www.zondervan.com/ebooks

Requests for information should be addressed to:
Zonderkidz, 5300 Patterson Ave. SE, Grand Rapids, Michigan 49530

Published in association with the literary agency of Alive Communications, Inc., 7680 Goddard Street, Suite 200, Colorado Springs, CO 80920. www.alivecommunucations.com

Zonderkidz is a trademark of Zondervan.

Interior art direction and design: Sarah Molegraaf
Cover illustrator: Steve James

Printed in the United States

13 14 15 16 17 18 19 / DCI / 24 23 22 21 20 19 18 17 16 15 14 13 12 11 10 9 8 7 6 5 4 3 2

So we fix our eyes not on what is seen,
but on what is unseen.
For what is seen is temporary,
but what is unseen is eternal.

—2 Corinthians 4:18

Sophie's World

One

"Sophie—hel-lo-o! I'm speaking to you!" *I know,* thought Sophie LaCroix, *but could you please stop? I can hardly think what to do next! Here I am in a strange country—I can't seem to find my trunk, and—*

"Sophie! Answer me!"

And could you please not call me "Sophie"? I'm Antoinette—from France.

"Are you all right?"

Sophie felt hands clamp onto her elf-like shoulders, and she looked up into the frowning face of Ms. Quelling, her sixth-grade social studies teacher. Sophie blinked her M&M-shaped eyes behind her glasses and sent the imaginary Antoinette scurrying back into her mind-world.

"Are you all right?" Ms. Quelling said again.

"Yes, ma'am," Sophie said.

"Then why didn't you answer me? I thought you were going into a coma, child." Ms. Quelling gave a too-big sigh. "Why do I even plan field trips?"

Sophie wasn't sure whether to answer that or not. She had only been in Ms. Quelling's class a month. In fact, she'd only been in Great Marsh Elementary School for a month.

"So answer my question," Ms. Quelling said. "Do you or don't you have a buddy in your group?"

"No, ma'am," Sophie said. She wasn't quite sure who was even *in* her field trip group.

"You're in the Patriots' Group." Ms. Quelling frowned over her clipboard, the skin between her eyebrows twisting into a backwards S. "Everybody in that group has a buddy except Maggie LaQuita—so I guess that's a no-brainer. Maggie, Sophie is your buddy. LaQuita and LaCroix, you two can be the La-La's."

Ms. Quelling rocked her head back and forth, sending her thick bronze hair bouncing off the sides of her face. She looked *very* pleased with her funny self.

But the stocky, black-haired girl who stepped up to them didn't seem to think it was the least bit hilarious. Sophie recognized Maggie from language arts class. She drilled her deep brown eyes into Ms. Quelling and then into Sophie.

Don't look at me, Sophie wanted to say out loud. *I don't want to be La-La either. I am Antoinette!*

Although, Sophie thought, *this Maggie person could fit right in. She looks like she's from a faraway kingdom, maybe Spain or some other romantic land. She can't be "Maggie" though,* Sophie decided. *She had to be Magdalena, a runaway princess.*

Magdalena glanced over her shoulder as she knelt to retrieve the leather satchel, stuffed with her most precious possessions—

"So are you getting on the bus or what?"

Maggie's voice dropped each word with a thud. She hiked her leather backpack over her shoulder and gave Sophie a push in the back that propelled tiny Sophie toward the steps.

"Sit here," Maggie said.

She shoved Sophie into a seat three rows back from the driver and fell in beside her. In front of them, the other four

Patriots fell into seats and stuffed their backpacks underneath. They twisted and turned to inspect the bus. Somebody's mother stood in the aisle with Ms. Quelling and counted heads.

"I have my six Patriots!" she sang out, smiling at their teacher. "Two boys, four girls!"

"Eddie and Colton, settle down!" Ms. Quelling said to the boys seated between the two pairs of girls. Eddie burrowed his knuckles into Colton's ball cap, and Colton grabbed the spike of sandy hair rising from Eddie's forehead.

"Dude," Maggie muttered. "I'm stuck in the loser group again."

Sophie squinted at Maggie. "I thought we were the Patriots."

"They just call us that so we won't *know* we're in the loser group."

"Oh," Sophie said.

She craned her neck to see over Colton and Eddie's heads and get a look at the other two Patriots. The girl with butter-blonde hair squirmed around in her seat to gaze longingly toward the back of the bus.

SHE hates being in the loser group too, Sophie thought. Actually she was pretty sure the girl, whose name she knew was B.J., hadn't lost anything but her usual knot of friends. She and three other girls always walked together as if they were attached with superglue.

B.J.'s lower lip stuck out like the seat of a sofa. Next to her sat a girl with a bouncy black ponytail. Ponytail Girl tugged at the back of B.J.'s T-shirt that read *Great Marsh Elementary School* — the same maroon one all of them were wearing. Sophie had selected a long skirt with daisies on it to wear with hers, as well as her hooded sweatshirt. She always felt most like Antoinette when she was wearing a hood.

B.J. leaned farther into the aisle. The only thing holding her onto the seat was the grip Ponytail Girl had on her.

"B.J., you're going to be on the floor any minute," said Chaperone Mom. "How about you scoot yourself right back up next to Kitty?"

"What?" B.J. said. She whirled around to Kitty and yanked her shirt away.

"B.J., what's the problem?" Ms. Quelling said from farther down the aisle.

B.J.'s sofa lip extended into a foldout couch. "If I could just be with my friends in the Colonists' Group—"

"And if ants could just have machine guns, we wouldn't step on them!" Ms. Quelling said.

"But they don't," Maggie said.

"Exactly." Ms. Quelling stretched her neck at B.J. over the top of the clipboard pressed to her chest. "I separated you because y'all talk too much, and you won't hear a word your guide says. You show me my best B.J., and we'll see about next time." She smiled like she and B.J. were old pals. "You can start by hiking yourself onto the seat before you break your neck."

As Ms. Quelling moved down the aisle, Chaperone Mom stepped into her place.

"Maybe you'll make some *new* friends today, B.J.," she said.

"I'll be your friend!" Kitty piped up.

B.J. glanced at her over her shoulder. "No offense or anything," she said. "But I already *have* friends."

Chaperone Mom gasped. "Now, that isn't nice!" She patted B.J. on the head and continued down the aisle.

"Busted," said Colton, wiggling his ears at B.J. Eddie let out a guffaw, and Colton punched him in the stomach.

"Boys are so lame," Maggie said. Her words placed themselves in a solid straight line, like fact blocks you couldn't possibly knock over. She looked at Sophie. "How come you hardly ever say anything?"

Sophie pulled her hood over her head, in spite of the Virginia-humid air. She wasn't sure when she could have squeezed a word into the conversation. Besides, she'd been too busy trying to figure out the possibilities.

Possibilities such as, *what does "B.J." stand for? Bambi Jo? Probably more like Bad Jerky.* B.J. looked as if she had just eaten some and was about to cough it back up.

And what about that Kitty person with the freckles? She must be Katherine, kept locked away in a tower, and she's so desperate to escape she clings to anyone she can reach. I'll save you! Rescue is my mission in life!

Antoinette tucked her long tresses beneath the hood of her dark cloak as she crept to the castle wall and gazed up at the tower.

"What are you looking at?"

Maggie's voice dropped on Sophie's daydream like a cement block. Sophie blinked at the bus ceiling above her.

"You think it's going to rain in here or what?" Maggie said. "I think you're a little strange."

"That's okay," Sophie said as she pushed back her hood. "Most people think I'm strange. My sister says I'm an alien from Planet Weird."

"Is that your real voice?" Maggie said.

Sophie didn't have a chance to tell her that, yes, the pip-squeak voice was the real thing, because the bus lurched forward and all its occupants squealed.

"Colonial Williamsburg, here we come!" Chaperone Mom shouted over the squeal-a-thon.

B.J. whirled again, her eyes fixed on the back of the bus like a jealous cat's.

Sophie turned to the window and curled her feet under her. As she watched the yellowing late September trees flip by in a blur, a heavy feeling fell over her head and shoulders, almost like a cloak—and *not* Antoinette's beautiful black velvet cape that shrouded her in soft mysterious folds from the dangers of the night.

This cloak felt like it was woven of sadness, and Sophie had been wearing it for six whole weeks, ever since her family had moved from Houston to the small town of Poquoson, Virginia.

Houston was a *huge* city with parks and museums and *big* libraries full of dream possibilities. Poquoson was mostly one street with a Farm Fresh grocery store and a Krispy Kreme Donut shop attached to a gas station, where hordes of mosquitoes flew through solid clouds of bug spray to gnaw on Sophie's legs.

The school was way different too. Here, Sophie had to change classes for every single subject, and that made it hard to keep up. It seemed as if she would just get settled into her seat in one classroom, when the bell sent her running to the next one, hauling her backpack, and leaving her work unfinished.

Of course, her new teachers had already told her—*and* her parents—that if she didn't stare out the window and daydream so much, she could get her work done before the end of class. In Houston the other students were used to her going off into daydreams. She hardly ever got teased about it there. But then her dad got promoted by NASA and moved the whole family to Virginia.

So the staring and taunting had started all over again since school started. This field trip was the first thing that even sounded like fun since they'd left Texas.

"Won't Williamsburg be amazing?" Sophie said to Maggie.

"No. Walking on the moon would be amazing. This is just historical."

Sophie sighed. "I wish it were French history. I want to learn about that. I'm into France."

Maggie pulled her chin in. "France? This is America."

"Is it?" Colton said. "Is it really? Hey, Eddie! This is America!"

"Huh?"

Colton gave him a left hook. "Maggot just said this is America. I thought we were in China, man."

"Don't call me maggot," Maggie said.

Sophie pulled her knees into a hug. Although her family hadn't had a chance to explore yet, Sophie's mother had collected brochures about the places they would go and had put Colonial Williamsburg at the top of the pile.

"They've restored one whole area so it looks just the way it was before and during the American Revolution," Mama had told her. "They say it's like stepping right back into the past."

"How long till we get there?" Sophie said. Maggie didn't answer. She whacked Colton with his own baseball cap, threw it at him, and then threatened both boys with their lives if they didn't stop calling her maggot.

"It isn't nice to hit boys," Chaperone Mom said. "It isn't nice to hit anybody."

"Why should I be nice to them?" Maggie said. "They sure aren't nice to me."

Sophie once again stared along the dense woods lining the highway and saw a sign appear, reading, "Colonial

Williamsburg." It had a little green shield on it, and Sophie felt a familiar flutter in her chest. This was real! It had its own little green shield and everything.

Sophie didn't hear Chaperone Mom's answer to Maggie. She geared up her imagination for an adventure—one that didn't include maggots or lame boys or anything not "nice" at all.

Two

"My name is Vic!" the skinny tour guide said. He had a smile like a slice of watermelon, and it seemed to Sophie that he ended every sentence with an exclamation point. "Follow me and stay together!"

The Patriots' Group followed Vic across the brick bridge that led away from the Williamsburg Visitors' Center. Sophie scanned the cobblestone and brick streets for a place Antoinette might appear. Maggie's foot smashed down the back of Sophie's sneaker. *I didn't think being field trip buddies meant we had to be Siamese twins*, Sophie thought. She picked up speed.

They passed along the side of a massive brick building with a curving wall and stopped in front of a tall iron gate. "This is the Governor's Palace!" Vic informed them. "Several royal governors lived here, including Governor Alexander Spotswood—not a very nice character!"

Surely there's a place for Antoinette beyond these gates, Sophie thought. She squirmed through the Patriots to get a closer view. Those high walls held who-knew-*what* amazing secrets. But with Colton and Eddie howling and B.J. repeating "What?" over and over, Sophie couldn't even FIND Antoinette.

"We'll visit the Governor's Palace at the end of your tour!" Vic said. Sophie caught up to him and gave the palace a wistful, backward glance as they walked along, right in the middle of the street.

"Where are the cars?" she said.

Vic looked down at her with the same surprised expression most adults made when they heard her speak for the first time. "Young lady," he answered, "you will find the Duke of Gloucester Street precisely as you would have in the eighteenth century!"

I love that! Sophie thought. At that very moment, a carriage rumbled past, driven by a man wearing white stockings, a coat with tails, and a three-cornered hat. Sophie closed her eyes and listened to the *clip-clop* of the horses' hooves.

Antoinette LaCroix peeked from inside the carriage, her face half hidden by the hood of her cloak. All around her colonists hurried to and fro, calling to each other in English. She could understand them, but how she longed to hear her native French.

"Hey!"

Something smacked Sophie on the top of the head. She blinked at Maggie, who was holding her map rolled up like a billy club.

"Come on," Maggie said. "You're supposed to stay with the group." She dragged Sophie forward by the wrist to where the group stood on tiptoes at a cemetery wall.

"This is Bruton Parish Church!" Vic said. "We'll visit here on our way back too!"

"Will we get to look at the graves?" Maggie said.

"Gross!" B.J. said. "Who wants to look at dead people?"

"Tombstones here date back to the 1600s!" Vic said, walking backward and beckoning the group with both hands. Sophie felt a delighted shiver.

Next they stopped in front of the courthouse. A man in a sweeping waistcoat and white silk stockings emerged through the tall wooden doors and shouted, "Nathaniel Buttonwick! Appear before the judge, or you will forfeit your recognizance!"

"What?" B.J. and Kitty said together.

Sophie didn't have any idea what *recognizance* meant either, but she loved the sound of it. Outside the courthouse two guards pushed a man's head through a hole in a wooden contraption and lowered a wooden railing over the man's wrists.

"In the stocks till sundown!" one guard shouted.

"He has to stand there until dark?" Sophie said.

"It's not real," Maggie said.

Antoinette was appalled. She had never seen such treatment, not in the gentle place from whence she came. Had it been a mistake to come to the colonies? But Antoinette shook her head until her tresses tossed against her face. She must find her mission.

Sophie wished she had a costume—like that little girl she saw across the street pushing a rolling hoop with a stick. She had on a white puffy cap and an apron-covered dress down to her ankles and white stockings that Sophie longed to feel on her own legs. A boy chased after her, trying to knock over her hoop.

I guess boys have always been annoying, Sophie thought. She caught up with Vic in time to hear that the powder magazine—an eight-sided brick building with a roof like a pointy hat—had once stored the cannons and guns and ammunition of Colonial Williamsburg's small army.

Sophie wanted to skip as they passed through an opening in the fence. A man with a big barrel chest suddenly blocked their path and bellowed, "Halt!"

"What?" B.J. and Kitty said.

21

"It's not real," Maggie said again, although she looked up at the giant of a man with reluctant respect in her eyes.

The man's tan shirt was the size of a pup tent, and the white scarf tied around his massive head framed a snarling face. Sophie swallowed hard.

"Fall in!" he shouted.

Colton fell to the ground, sending Eddie into a fit of boy-howls.

"That means fall into a straight line!"

The rest of them scrambled into place. The big man picked Colton up by his backpack and set him down on his feet next to Sophie.

"Hey, dude!" Colton said.

"You will call me Sergeant! Let me hear it!"

"Yes, Sergeant!" Sophie cried out.

Eddie went into convulsions of laughter. Colton said, "Yes, Sergeant," in a mousy voice.

"You—and you—fall out!" the sergeant roared.

Eddie and Colton were banished to a blue wagon full of long poles, where the sergeant told them to stay until further notice. When Chaperone Mom started to march over to them, the sergeant yelled, "You! Fall in!"

"Oh, no, I'm the chaperone!" she said.

"We need every able-bodied individual! We are no longer a small militia—we are part of the Colonial Army! If Lafayette and his troops do not arrive in time, it will be us against the Redcoats!"

Lafayette? Sophie thought. *That sounds like a French name.*

"Eyes left! Eyes front! Eyes left!" the sergeant commanded. When he said, "Pick up your arms!" the group scurried for the blue wagon and got their "guns"—long sticks almost twice as tall as Sophie. The sergeant told Eddie and Colton that he would give them one last chance, and they grabbed their sticks to line up with the rest.

"Left flank!" the sergeant cried, and he showed them how to stand their guns along their left legs. Then he taught them how to "load," how to shift from "flank" to "shoulder," how to "make ready" and "present" in one smooth motion, and to "make fire" only when he commanded. At those words, everyone screamed, "Boom!"

Antoinette had never held a weapon before in her life, but if this was what it took to fulfill her mission, then she could do it.

"Make ready!" the sergeant cried.

With her musket firmly in her hands, Antoinette dropped to her knee, waiting for the commands to present and fire.

"You! You there, soldier!"

Sophie looked into the sergeant's face and clung to her stick. "Yes, Sergeant?" she said.

"You're a fine soldier. You shame the whole lot of them. You can fight in my company anytime."

"Thank you, Sergeant," Sophie said.

Afterward, Sophie floated happily down the street with the Patriots. She was now a part of Colonial Williamsburg—one of its finest soldiers.

"Hey, pipsqueak," Colton said to her.

Sophie glared at him. "That's *Corporal* Pipsqueak to you, *Private*."

"What's she talking about?" Eddie said.

"Nothing," Colton said. "She's whacked."

But right by Vic's elbow, with Maggie walking up her calves, Sophie felt anything but whacked as she made Williamsburg her own.

Inside the houses and shops, every detail swept her back across the centuries: a powdered wig on a dressing table, a quill pen in a china holder, and a four-poster bed with mosquito netting draped down its sides. *I want that in MY bedroom*, Sophie thought.

The formal English gardens with clipped hedges helped her picture Antoinette waiting among the flowers for the delivery of a secret message. And the little brick pathways covered in ivy leading down from the streets were custom-made for Antoinette's getaways.

She loved it *all*, including the sign above the jeweler's that said, "Engraving. Watch-Making. Done in the Beft Manner."

"Beft?" Sophie said.

Of course, B.J. said, "What?"

"Best," Maggie told her.

Sophie decided to start writing all of her *S*'s that way from now on. She felt certain that Lafayette, whoever he was, had made his *S*'s just like that.

When they stopped to have a picnic in the Market Square, Sophie inched close to Vic.

"Could you tell me about Lafayette?" she said.

"The Marquis de Lafayette was a young French nobleman," Vic said. "Red-headed, very short, and small-boned. He was only nineteen years old when he bought a ship and left France secretly to help the Colonists. Without him, the patriots might not have won the war, and we wouldn't be free today."

"He *bought* a whole ship?" Colton said. "He must've had cash."

"Lafayette used his wealth to help the American colonies because he believed in fairness," Vic said. "All his life he stood against anything that was more evil than good."

"So did he make it to Williamsburg in time?" Sophie said. "The sergeant said if he didn't get here with his troops, the militia would be on its own."

Vic gave her his big watermelon smile. "You were paying attention!"

"I was too!" B.J. muttered to Kitty. They gave Sophie identical narrow-eyed stares.

"So did he get here in time?" Sophie said.

"He did! But there was almost disaster."

Sophie felt the flutter in her chest. Disaster always had possibilities.

"Lafayette moved his advance units to about ten miles north of here. Someone gave him false information—that most of the British Army had already crossed the James River. So he decided to move closer to Jamestown and attack whatever enemy troops remained."

"But the whole British Army was still there!" Sophie said.

"So did the Brits waste him?" Colton said.

"No," Vic said. "He learned about the trap and marched straight to Yorktown, where the war was won."

"Who told him about the trap?" Maggie said.

But Sophie didn't listen to the answer.

From her hiding place in the Market Square, Antoinette held her breath until the British Loyalists moved on. She didn't breathe from the time she heard their secret plans until she was sure they had gone into the Raleigh Tavern. Then she gathered up her skirts and ran for the carriage house. She had to reach the Marquis de Lafayette with the news—before he marched right into the British trap.

"Hey! Sophie!"

"*What?*" Sophie said.

She shook off the hand that Maggie had wrapped around her backpack strap.

"Fine," Maggie said. Her eyes narrowed into fudge-colored slits. "I won't tell you that everybody else is going shopping." She put up her hands. "You're way too high-maintenance."

As she stomped away, Sophie squinted at the rest of the Patriots gathered under a canvas souvenir shelter, pawing through toy muskets and Revolutionary flags. Sophie saw B.J. put something white on her head and make a face at Kitty.

That's one of those puffy caps! Sophie thought. She raced toward the tent. She ran her fingers along the three-cornered hats and white stockings and full dresses with aprons. Those, she discovered, were way too expensive, so she settled for a white cap in a bin that said "Mobcaps."

"Are you actually going to *buy* one of those?" B.J. asked.

"B.J., be nice," Chaperone Mom said. "She just wants a souvenir, don't you, honey?"

Sophie shook her head. "No. I want it for a game I'm going to act out."

B.J. stared with her mouth open as if Sophie had just announced she was having plastic surgery. Sophie knew that look, and she could almost hear her thirteen-year-old sister Lacie in her head:

Sophie, you can play your little games. Just don't tell anyone you're doing it. Keep it to yourself or they'll think you're totally from Planet Weird.

Sure enough, B.J. exchanged raised-eyebrow looks with Kitty.

"All right, Patriots!" Vic called out. "Complete your purchases and let's go!"

Sophie paid for a ballpoint quill pen and her cap. She tucked the pen carefully into her backpack and placed the cap on her head. Then she followed the group toward the Capitol Building. This time Sophie didn't hurry to catch up with Vic, because Kitty and B.J. flanked him, and Maggie hadn't returned to drag her along. Sophie felt the cloak of sadness descend on her shoulders.

But I haven't the time to feel sorry for myself, Antoinette thought. *I must get word to Lafayette. The fate of the militia is at stake!* Glancing over both shoulders to make sure the British were nowhere in sight, Antoinette straightened her white lacy cap. She hurried down a set of stone steps and ran between the shops. *It would be best to stay out of sight just in case they suspected her.*

Behind her the sound of horse-drawn carriages faded, and she hurried through a maze of hedges in a garden behind the hat shop, and then she hoisted herself over a brick wall. Antoinette stopped to catch her breath. *This is a graveyard!* She put her hand over her mouth.

And so did Sophie.

Sophie scanned the rows of tombstones. The rest of the Patriots were nowhere in sight.

Three

O h no," Sophie said to the nearest gravestone. "I'm lost."

Usually the idea of being lost had great possibilities. But right now, Sophie's heart pounded. Ms. Quelling would make the eyebrow face. Mama would say, "I'm so disappointed." And Daddy—

Sophie squeezed her eyes shut. *I have to find a way to get found!* Straightening her mobcap, Sophie ran along a dirt path through the tombstones to a large brick building. The front door opened, and a man in a necktie led a group of grownups down the steps. Sophie hung back as the man began to speak. "Please take the time to look around the church cemetery," he said. "You'll find markers dating back to the early seventeenth century."

Oh, this is that church! Sophie thought. She remembered that the Patriots' Group would have to pass this way to see the Governor's Palace. *I'll just wait for them here*, she decided. *I hope Chaperone Mom doesn't start yelling about how not nice I am, right here in the cemetery.*

"Welcome to Bruton Parish Church, ladies and gentlemen," said Necktie Man to a new group near the steps. "We ask you to please keep your voices low in the church, as this is an active place of worship and there may be people praying inside."

Sophie hitched up her backpack and hurried to join them. Chaperone Mom might yell out *here*, but Mr. Necktie wouldn't let her raise her voice in *there*.

When she stepped inside, the church itself seemed to whisper, "Shhh!"

At the end of each church pew stood a small door, so that the pews formed long narrow cubicles. Sophie slipped inside one and closed its door as Mr. Necktie filed past with his tour.

I'll hide here until I hear Vic, she decided. *If Maggie hasn't informed on me yet, I can just sneak right back into the group, and it'll be just fine.* She let out a long, slow breath and looked up at the pulpit where the minister probably preached his sermons. It looked like it was suspended in midair. *That looks high enough for Jesus to preach from*, Sophie thought.

Sometimes in church when sermons got boring, Sophie liked to imagine that Jesus himself was talking. She knew stories from Sunday school, and she'd heard people talking about what Jesus would do, so she could imagine him saying some words. But the *picture* she held of him in her mind felt *very* clear.

His kind eyes never narrowed into slits or rolled into his head like he thought she was whacked. He had a real smile too, one that couldn't switch into a curled-up lip. His whole face understood what it was like to imagine amazing things and act them out, even when every *other* girl in the galaxy was acting like she was poison ivy.

"Jesus," she whispered. "I don't think you'd yell at me just because I got wrapped up with Antoinette and got lost. I think you'd understand me." She sighed. "But Jesus—it would *really* help if I had just one friend *here* who understood me too, and we could imagine stuff together, and I wouldn't feel so lonely all the time. Do you think I could have that, please?"

She looked up at the pulpit again. *Don't be up there,* she prayed. *I wish you were here next to me and I wasn't in trouble and you wouldn't let them be mad at me.*

Someone cleared his throat and Mr. Necktie peered over her pew door. Only then did Sophie realize she was actually on her knees. "Miss, I didn't want to disturb your prayer—"

But the pew door flew open with a bang, and Ms. Quelling said in a louder-than-prayer voice, "*You* have some explaining to do."

Sophie wondered why Ms. Quelling always asked for an explanation, because she never gave her a chance to give one. Even though Sophie had to sit next to her in the front seat of the bus all the way back to Poquoson, the teacher obviously wanted Sophie to keep her explanations to herself.

And when they got off the bus, Ms. Quelling gave Sophie's mother her *own* version of the story, as if Sophie had spent the entire trip planning how to ruin everybody's day.

"It wasn't like that, Mama," Sophie said as they left the school in the Suburban.

"I know it wasn't," Mama said. "I think she's just a little upset." She looked at Sophie with her brown-like-Sophie's eyes. "And I can imagine she was terrified that something had happened to you." Mama tilted her head in that elf-like way she had, her frosty curls slipping to the side. "Soph, I know you didn't do it on purpose, but we have to make sure this doesn't happen again."

When they pulled into the driveway of their two-story gray house, Sophie's older sister, Lacie, was kicking a soccer ball to five-year-old Zeke in the front yard. Lacie and Zeke ran to the car. Neither of them had Sophie's soft voice.

"Mama, can we have the cookies now?" Zeke said.

Lacie stared at Sophie. "What's that thing on your head?" she said.

Sophie ignored them, ran into the house, and flew up the shiny wooden stairs that turned a corner on their way. She hurled herself into her room, closed the door behind her, and tossed her backpack aside.

Circling the bed, she flicked on her table lamp with the princess base and leaned against the white bookcase by the window that looked into the arms of an oak tree. Sophie wrapped her fingers around the gauzy curtains and shut her eyes.

Antoinette pulled the mosquito netting around her shoulders. She knew it wouldn't hide her from Governor Spotswood when he came thundering through the library door, but for now she must order her mind. How can I explain to him why I was dashing off into the woods? I can't tell him that I was helping Lafayette! The governor is a Loyalist. They'll put me in the stocks. Or worse—

There was an impatient knock. *Before Antoinette could say, "Come in," the library door flew open.*

Sophie peeked one eye between the gauzy curtains as Daddy came through the door. He looked taller and more big-shouldered than ever.

"Come in, sir," Sophie said.

"Sir?" Daddy said. For a second a twinkle shot through one of his blue eyes.

"In Williamsburg, we had to call the sergeant 'sir'—"

The twinkle disappeared.

"I guess Mama told you what happened," Sophie said.

"She did." Daddy pulled up the pink vanity stool and sat carefully on it. "What were you thinking, Soph?"

"I was thinking about a story I was making up," Sophie said. "And then all of a sudden, my group was gone. I guess I got carried away."

He blinked and ran his hand through his thick black hair. "At least you're honest."

I hope that counts when you start thinking up my punishment, Sophie thought.

"But you give me the same reason every time something like this happens."

"I couldn't help it," Sophie said. "You should see that place. Everything is exactly like it was back in the olden days—*exactly*!"

"They make it that way so you can learn your history—not so you can get so caught up in the fantasy of it that you wander off. Can you promise me that this won't happen again?"

Sophie thought about it, and then she shook her head.

"Why not?"

"Because—it just happens."

"And is it the same thing that 'just happens' when you stare into space in the classroom and don't get your work done?"

"Yes, sir."

Daddy's eyebrows pinched together. "Then we have to find a way to make it stop happening," he said.

There was a light tap on the door and Mama slipped in. She perched on the edge of Sophie's bed, her feet dangling above the floor.

"We're just talking about how we're going to stop all this daydreaming," Daddy said.

You were just talking about it, Sophie thought. *I don't want to stop daydreaming.*

"I guess we're going to have to go with what we talked about," he said.

What is this? Sophie thought. *Are they going to put me in the stocks or what?*

"Okay," Daddy said to her. "As soon as we can get you in, you're going to start seeing a counselor. Your mother will fill you in on all the details."

Sophie thought her eyes were going to pop out of her head. "A counselor?" she said. "You mean, like a psychiatrist?"

"No!" Mama said. "He's a counselor you can talk to." She reached across and touched Sophie's cheek. "We know you're unhappy, Dream Girl."

"And he helps kids straighten out so they can do better in school." Daddy sat up straight. "And you *have* to promise, Sophie, that you will try to do everything he says. Am I clear?"

"Yes, sir," Sophie said.

When her parents had closed the door behind them, Sophie flounced across her pillows, hair streaming.

"Please," Antoinette cried to the governor. *"Please don't send me to that awful place. I'm not crazy! I have a mission to accomplish!"*

"Are you nuts?"

Sophie looked up miserably at Lacie, whose compact frame stood in the doorway, still in her soccer clothes.

"They think I am," Sophie said. "And don't you know how to knock?" She flung both arms out to her sides.

"Okay, lose the drama." Lacie scooped her dark-like-Daddy's hair into a ponytail holder she'd been wearing on her wrist. "Do you *want* to go see this shrink?"

"No! He's just gonna tell me I'm weird like everybody else does, and my grades are still going to be bad, and Daddy will ground me forever, and then I'll have to sit here like I'm in prison—"

"Not that you wouldn't actually enjoy the drama." Lacie's face took on the sharp look that made her freckles fold into stern little dashes. "You want some advice?"

Like I could stop you, Sophie wanted to say.

"You need something to do," Lacie said. "So you won't even think about daydreaming."

"I don't want to play soccer, if that's what you're going to say."

"It doesn't have to be soccer. It can be volleyball or softball—"

"I'm not good at sports."

"Okay, so chess—no, not chess. That's for brainy kids."

"I'm not stupid!"

"I'm not either. I make straight A's—remember?"

Sophie sniffed. *As if you* or *Daddy ever let me forget it.*

"It's cool to make good grades if you handle it right," Lacie said. "You're smart enough if you'll just focus. You don't focus because you're off on Planet Weird, so you need something that you can think about—something in the real world."

That's just it, Sophie thought. *Sometimes I don't even like the real world.*

"You only *think* you're not good at sports," Lacie said. "Let me work with you on some basic skills."

"N.O.!"

Lacie scrunched up one eye and put her finger in her ear. "Okay, okay! Why do you have to do that? You about pierced my eardrum. A simple 'no' would do."

"Would it get you out of my room?" Sophie said.

"Probably."

"Then—simply *no.*"

"All right. Fine." Lacie folded her arms across her chest the way Daddy did. "I'm just trying to help you so you won't become a total loser. Just promise me you aren't going to wear that stupid white cap to school."

"I thought you said a simple 'no' would get you out of my room."

"I'm going. I'm just telling you—"

Sophie readied for another high-pitched squeal. Lacie raced out the door.

Antoinette sighed under the mosquito netting. If it weren't for her mission to save Lafayette, she would fire Lacette, that saucy little maidservant. Then she would flee this miserable place. She would board a ship and sail triumphantly back to Paris, where they understood her for the hero she really was.

The next morning in language arts, Maggie passed Sophie a note that said, "So did you get busted?" Sophie wrote back with her quill pen: *Yef. Bufted.*

Sophie counted every minute, trying to ignore Maggie and B.J. and her group who couldn't seem to talk about anything else BUT the incident on the field trip. In social studies, Ms. Quelling took her aside and said, "You can't hope for better than a C in citizenship after your stunt yesterday. Keep your mind on your work, and STOP making your *S*'s like *F*'s."

The misery went on for days. Every day, Sophie stopped at the cafeteria door just long enough to throw away her sandwich, and then she fled outside to meet Antoinette. About a week after the field trip, on a lonely Tuesday, she was on the top of the rusted monkey bars nobody ever used.

Antoinette didn't care about rust—or the stocks—or the advancing British soldiers. All she cared about was getting to Lafayette. His encampment lay just over the hill. She knew the troops were making ready to cross the James River, right into the trap. *Antoinette let her cloak fly out behind her as she grappled up the hill, ignoring the biting wind, fearless now of even Governor Spotswood himself. If she could just reach the top before—*

"Hey—where are you?"

Sophie had to twist to look under her own arm. A pair of wonderful gray eyes, set in a golden face, looked up at her. The girl tucked a strand of chocolate brown hair behind her ear, where it crept out again.

"Are you climbing a hill or a wall?" she said. Sophie had never seen the girl before, and she didn't dare believe her ears.

"Hill," she said finally.

"Who are you?" the girl said.

"Sophie LaCroix."

"I know that. I mean, who are you right now?"

"I'm Antoinette," Sophie said.

She waited for the eye roll, the curled lip, the "You are weird!"

"Oh," the girl said. "So—can I play?" Her eyes took on a dreamy glow. "I could be Henriette."

Four

Sophie stared with her mouth wide open as "Henriette" climbed to the bar below her.

"Are we French?" the girl whispered.

Sophie nodded.

"*Bonjour!*" the girl cried.

Sophie answered, "*Bonjour!*"

"*Merci, Mademoiselle Antoinette.* Why are we climbing this hill?"

Sophie sucked in her breath. Her answer might send "Henriette" racing across the playground yelling "Weirdo alert!" Sophie let out the breath.

"I must get a message to Lafayette," she said. "Or else he and his troops will walk into a trap—"

"You can't go alone! It's too dangerous! I'll keep watch for you."

Sophie squinted at her through her glasses. "Can you be trusted?"

"You have my word," said "Henriette" solemnly. "I can give you no greater guarantee than that."

Sophie fought back a smile of relief and nodded seriously, whispering, "All right, then. But stay low."

Behind them, Great Marsh Elementary School transformed into the maze of gardens and stone walls of Williamsburg, and the shouts of other students became those of the British, foiled in their attempt to trick the brave Marquis de Lafayette.

The Marquis bowed on one knee to kiss their hands.

"You brave damsels must allow me to repay you in some way."

"It is enough to know we have helped you," Antoinette said, her head bowed.

"Oui, monsieur," said Henriette.

"What are y'all doing up there?"

Sophie unfolded from her bow. Four faces stared up at them.

"This is what she was doing in Williamsburg, Julia," said B.J. "Being weird." She pointed at Sophie and nudged the tall girl.

Julia tucked in her chin. Her thick, russet ponytail fell forward. "*What* are y'all *doing*?" she said again.

"Imagining," said "Henriette." "What are *y'all* doing?"

A nervous-eyed girl with short, black hair let out a squeal that reminded Sophie of a toy poodle.

"We're being normal," Julia said. She glanced at her friends expectantly, and they all nodded. The giggly one cackled with B.J. and a fourth girl, who was so thin that Sophie felt certain she'd fall over if someone breathed on her. Skinny Girl ended with a loud, juicy sniff.

"Would you like a *serviette*?" said "Henriette."

Julia flipped an impatient hand through the air. "This is just way too weird."

She turned and strode off, ponytail swishing importantly from side to side. The other three followed her like ducks.

"I have two questions," Sophie said when they were gone.

"Number one," said "Henriette," holding up a finger.

"What's a *serviette*?"

"It's French for 'napkin.' She totally needed to blow her nose, but I don't know the word for Kleenex." She held up a second finger. "Number two?"

"What's your this-world name?"

"Fiona Bunting. Today's my first day."

Sophie swung down from the bars and dropped to the ground with Fiona right behind her.

"How did you know my name already, then?" Sophie said.

"I heard B.J. talking about you in class, so I asked her your name." Fiona rolled her wonderful gray eyes. "She said it was Soapy, and then she was all laughing. That's because she's a Pop—you know, a popular girl. They think every corny word out of their mouths is funny."

Sophie gave her a sideways glance. "You didn't think it was funny—what B.J. said?"

"No! I thought it was absolutely heinous."

"Heinous?" Sophie said.

"Dreadful. Wretched," said Fiona. "Heinous *far* exceeds horrible."

"Oh," said Sophie. "I understand you."

"Yeah," Fiona said, "and I understand you too."

For the rest of the week, Sophie and Fiona lived together in the world of Antoinette and Henriette. After lunch, after school—even on the phone after supper and almost all weekend—until Lacie complained to Daddy that Sophie was hogging the line. Mostly, for Sophie, it was about what Fiona called the deliciousness of it all. Some of it, though, helped her NOT to think about going to see the counselor on Monday.

During after-lunch free time that day, Sophie and Fiona were near the monkey bars. Sophie crouched on the ground beside Fiona, holding her hand and stroking her forehead.

"*Now* what are y'all doing?"

Sophie tried to ignore the sound of Julia's voice. Henriette had scarlet fever—this was no time for conversation.

"Hello? Anybody home?"

Sophie finally looked up at her least favorite faces on the playground.

Fiona groaned, "Must you be so imperious, Julia?"

"What?" B.J. said. Kitty hovered around B.J. like a moth, echoing "What?" and sending the giggly girl into poodle shrieks.

"Willoughby—Kitty—shut *up*," Julia said.

"We're playing a game," Fiona said.

"I *know* that," Julia said.

Fiona blinked her gray eyes. "Then why did you ask?"

"Well," Julia said, "because you're lying on the ground and Soapy is patting your head like you're a cocker spaniel."

That sent Willoughby into a fresh batch of giggles.

"Willoughby!" Julia said, snapping her red braid like a whip. "I told you to shut *up*!"

"I can't help it," Willoughby said. "Her voice makes me laugh."

"Yours doesn't make *me* laugh," Julia said.

Willoughby whimpered and hid behind the shoulder of the skinny blonde.

"You should get up off the ground, Fiona," the skinny girl said. Her voice was thick, as if she still had nose problems.

"Tell me why, Anne-Stuart," Fiona said to the skinny girl. "Is there a *rule* against lying down outside?"

"There ought to be," Julia said. "There ought to be a rule against being weird, period."

"But who says what's weird and what's not?" Fiona said.

Sophie gaped at her friend. Fiona sure enjoyed an argument. Sophie usually just shrugged and went back into her daydreams when stuff like this happened. They only had about five more minutes of free time to bring Henriette back to health, and she didn't want to waste it on the Pops.

"Everybody knows it's weird to still be playing make believe in the *sixth grade*," B.J. said. "That's like a rule itself."

"Everybody knows it," Kitty chimed in. "I even know it."

"That's why everybody thinks you're strange, Sophie," Anne-Stuart said. "If you acted, you know, like normal, you'd have more friends."

Fiona propped herself up on her elbows. "Would *you* be our friend, Anne-Stuart?"

"I am so over this," Julia said, and led her train of Pops away.

Fiona lifted her face closer to Sophie's. "I didn't *think* she wanted us in her little group."

"Whatever," Sophie said. She flopped back onto her elbows. She could feel herself scowling.

"Are you mad at me?" Fiona said.

"No," Sophie said. "I just wish I didn't have to go where I have to go this afternoon."

"Orthodontist?"

"No." Sophie pulled a strand of her hair under her nose like a moustache. "Do you promise you won't tell another single solitary person about this? Not now or ever."

Fiona's eyes went round. "I promise on Henriette's soul," she said. "What's up?"

"I have to go see a psychiatrist," Sophie whispered.

Fiona sat straight up. "No way! My parents tried that on me too."

"Then—what do you think he's going to be like? I can't even imagine it—and I can imagine just about anything!"

Fiona rolled onto her belly and rested her chin in her hands. "He'll be old and bald and definitely crazier than you, but don't worry. Even though it's heinous at first, it won't last long."

"It won't?" Sophie said.

"No." Fiona looked wise. "See, the thing with psychiatrists is that if they're going to change you, you have to *want* to change. Both my therapists told me that first thing. When I told them I didn't want to change, they told my parents they couldn't do anything for me."

Sophie sagged. "I can't do that. I promised my father that I would try to do everything the counselor told me."

Fiona gave an elaborate sigh and fell back into Henriette's deathbed.

"Then I suppose our fun is over," she said. She flung her arm across her forehead.

"No, Henriette!" Antoinette cried. "Nothing will ever come between us. Not the British! Not that evil doctor! Nothing!"

Nothing except the bell.

"Don't let them change you," Fiona said as they jogged toward the building. "Don't let them."

That afternoon, Sophie trudged toward the old Suburban with her sadness cloak so heavy that she could barely lift herself into the front seat.

From the back, Zeke shouted, "Hey, Mama!" Her little brother always yelled as though he stood at the opposite end of a soccer field.

Sophie turned to look at him. His dark, thick hair stood in spikes, and his eyebrows wobbled up and down.

"You know what about Spider-Man?"

While Mama cooed over something Zeke had told her about a hundred and three times, Sophie stared glumly out the window.

I don't get it, she thought. *Zeke thinks Spider-Man is real. He thinks he IS Spider-Man or Peter Parker or whoever and nobody sends him off to a psychiatrist. I know Antoinette is only in my mind, but everybody thinks I'm a nut case. And now I have to go try to explain that to some stranger.*

She sighed all the way from the hollow in her stomach. This was heinous. Absolutely heinous.

Five

The counselor was waiting when Mama, Zeke, and Sophie arrived. He wasn't what Sophie and Fiona had dreamed up—at *all*—with his short, gelled hair and his twinkly blue eyes behind rimless glasses. He didn't look even a little bit crazy.

"Hey, Sophie," he said, reaching to shake her hand. "I'm Peter Topping, but you can call me Dr. Peter if you want."

Zeke was obviously impressed, because he immediately launched into babble about the ice cream he was about to get if Sophie didn't cry while she was at the doctor. *Too bad* he *wasn't the one who had to stay,* Sophie thought.

"It's okay if she cries in *this* office," Dr. Peter said. "But I'll do my best not to *make* her cry."

But after Mama assured Sophie that she *and* Daddy would be back to get her, Sophie was sure she *would* start to cry the minute she followed Dr. Peter into a bright room.

"How about we sit over here?" Dr. Peter pointed to a long window seat in the corner.

"Yes, sir," Sophie said. She hiked herself up onto some plump cushions shaped like faces and folded her hands in her lap. Dr. Peter sat on the other end.

Just as he started to open his mouth, Sophie said, "Could I go first?"

"O—kay," he said, dragging out the O. "Sure—go for it."

She took in a huge breath. "I don't really want to change, so I don't know if you can help me. I told my dad that I would try to do whatever you told me, so I'm going to—but I don't want to. I just thought you should know that."

Dr. Peter didn't laugh. Nor did he throw up his hands and say, "Then there's nothing I can do for you." He just nodded and said, "I appreciate your being so honest with me. My turn?"

Sophie just nodded.

"I'm not going to try to change you," Dr. Peter said. "I couldn't if I wanted to, which I don't."

Sophie could feel her eyes widening. "Does my dad know that?"

"He will when I talk to your parents later this afternoon."

"So—then—what *are* you going to do to me?"

"I'm not going to do anything *to* you," Dr. Peter said. "I'm just going to help you discover how you can live the best life possible. Fair enough?"

Sophie wasn't sure. She pulled a strand of hair under her nose.

"That doesn't sound good to you?" he said.

"Not if I have to give up dreaming up stories and pretending I'm in them."

Dr. Peter snatched up a pillow, one with a huge, hooked nose protruding from it, and looked into its puffy eyes. "Would I try to make her do *that*?" he said.

The pillow shook its head no.

"No way," Dr. Peter said. "In fact—" He turned the pillow to face Sophie. "We want to hear these stories of yours."

45

Sophie let the strand of hair drop. "You do?" she said.

"I do."

"Are you going to laugh at them?"

"Are they funny?"

"Not to me."

"Then I won't laugh."

"Are you going to tell me my stories aren't real?" she said. "Because I already *know* that."

"Of course you do. Anything else?"

Sophie reached for her hair again. "I guess there's one more thing."

"Bring it on."

"Are you going to tell me I'm too old to play?"

Dr. Peter gave the hook-nosed pillow a befuddled look. "When is a person *ever* too old to play?"

"For real?" Sophie said.

"Let me tell you a secret," Dr. Peter said. He lowered his voice to a loud whisper. "One of the main reasons grown-ups have so many problems is because they've forgotten how to play."

Sophie nodded soberly. "I see your point."

"Good," Dr. Peter said. "Now, let's hear about these dreams of yours."

He settled back into the pillows, hugging the hook-nosed one to his chest. Sophie crossed her legs in front of her and told Dr. Peter all about Antoinette and Henriette, and through it all, Dr. Peter nodded and sometimes even asked a question—like "Is Antoinette tall?"

"Oh, no," Sophie told him. "She's very small for her age, kind of like me. That comes in handy sometimes, when she has to hide herself—you know—for a mission."

"Of course," Dr. Peter said. "And where do you and Fiona act out your stories?"

"Well, mostly on the old playground nobody uses anymore. But when it's raining in the mornings, sometimes we sneak behind the stage curtain in the cafeteria. It's dusty and dark and huge."

"Very appropriate. So tell me, how do Antoinette's parents feel about her mission?"

"They worry about the dangerous things she does, but they're secretly very proud of her—especially her father."

"As well he should be," Dr. Peter said. He glanced at the clock. "I wish we had more time—this is fascinating. But I need to ask you one more question."

"Bring it on," Sophie said. She snuggled into the face pillows behind her. A nose peeked out from under her arm.

"Why do you think your parents are so concerned about your having these wonderful dreams and acting them out?"

Sophie whipped out a piece of hair and dragged it under her nose again. "They—mostly my dad—think I'm too old for pretend. They want me to be like Lacie—that's my sister—and play sports and join clubs and make straight A's. Mostly it's about school."

"What about school?"

"I don't get my work done. And I don't always hear what the teachers are saying because I'm daydreaming."

"You sure are an honest client."

"I'm a client?" Sophie said. She liked the sound of that.

"You're my client, and I'm your advisor." He grinned at her. "And right now I'm only going to advise you to do one thing."

Here it comes, Sophie thought. She tried not to let her eyes glaze over.

"I don't want you to stop making up stories and acting them out. I'm going to talk to your parents about a different *way* for you to do that. But I want to wait to tell you until after I talk to them."

"They'll say no," Sophie said. "Daddy will, anyway."

"I think the only reason he'll say no is if he can't afford it, which is why I need to talk to him first. Do you trust me?"

"I guess I have to," she said.

Dr. Peter adjusted his glasses. "You don't *have* to do anything I advise you to do. You can make the choice."

"No, I can't. I promised my father I would try to do everything you told me to do."

"Tell you what," Dr. Peter said. "Since your father asked you to try, then you should. But you still have a choice; if it doesn't work for you, you can stop."

Sophie could feel her eyes narrowing. "Are you going to tell *him* that?"

"Definitely," Dr. Peter said.

She considered that for a moment, and then she pulled her hair under her nose again.

"Does the mustache mean you're not convinced?" Dr. Peter said.

"It means I don't think my dad is going to buy it."

"Why not?"

"Because he doesn't *get* me—not like he gets everybody else in the whole entire galaxy."

"Can you give me an example?"

Sophie didn't even have to think about it. "My little brother—you met him—Zeke?"

"Right."

"He's all into Spider-Man—he actually *believes* Spider-Man is real. My dad thinks that's hilarious—he even plays Spider-Man *with* him sometimes. But I *know* Antoinette isn't real, and my father sends me to a psychiatrist. No offense."

"None taken," Dr. Peter said, "because I'm not a psychiatrist— I'm a psychologist, which is very different. Just think of me as somebody you can talk to."

Sophie nodded.

"How about another example?"

Sophie resituated herself. "Okay—Mama. She's the most creative person in the *world*. She has her Loom Room over our garage, and she weaves fabric all by herself."

"So that's where you've inherited *your* creativity."

"But that's what I don't *get*!" Sophie said. "She uses her imagination—and Daddy is all proud of her. I use *my* imagination, and he thinks I'm too old for it!"

"You know what, Sophie?" Dr. Peter said. "There are probably some reasons for that—some of them good, some of them maybe not so good. I'm going to get right on that, though, okay?"

Sophie sat in the waiting room while Dr. Peter talked to her parents. She swung her legs and wished she knew what they were saying in there.

Madame LaCroix nodded gracefully as the great Dr. Pierre LaTopp described Antoinette's rare creative abilities. But Monsieur LaCroix sat in the corner with his arms folded across his chest and scowled. Antoinette knew what he was thinking. "Ridiculous!" But Antoinette did not despair. She knew the great doctor would make him understand. After all, Papa was proud of her. Secretly so proud.

Sophie let the dream-air puff from her lips. *I just want to be understood*, she thought. *Why can't I have that?*

Suddenly Sophie remembered thinking those words before. She had prayed the same thing in Bruton Parish Church. *Wow!* she thought with a jerk. *It happened! I have Fiona. That must be because of God!*

But what if Daddy and Mama won't let me keep Fiona after they talk to Dr. Peter because she's a dreamer like me? Sophie swung her legs harder. *What if they won't even let me keep Dr. Peter after he says he won't make me change?*

That would be heinous, she thought. *Because I think he might understand me too.*

Madame LaCroix came to her, holding out both hands, tears glistening in her eyes.

"I am so sorry, my precious daughter. How could I ever have asked you to give up your dreams?" Antoinette closed her eyes, *fighting back her own sobs. Now—could she even dare to hope that Papa would feel the same way?*

"You catching a nap, Soph?" her father asked.

Sophie opened her eyes to see Daddy standing over her.

"Do I get to keep Fiona as my friend?"

He looked completely confused. "Who's Fiona?"

Sophie took a deep breath. "I know Dr. Peter told you I can keep doing my stories, and you hate that, and you're going to make me stop, and Fiona won't play with me anymore, and she's the only friend I have, and if I have to give her up I'll curl up and die a miserable death."

Her dad stared. "Soph, that is the most bizarre train of logic I've ever heard. Does that actually make sense to you?"

"Darlin'," Mama said. "I'm so happy you have a friend and that she's somebody you feel comfortable with." She looked at Daddy. "We never said you couldn't play with your friends."

"As long as you don't—" But Daddy stopped when Mama nudged him with her elbow. Sophie felt her hands going clammy. She had never seen them disagree about one of the kids.

"We want to make a deal with you." Daddy put on what Sophie knew was his game face. "Dr. Topping thinks it would be a good idea for you to record your stories with a video camera. You can act them out and record them—instead of dreaming them up during class. At least that way, you're getting something practical out of it. It won't hurt to learn how to use a camera."

"You mean like a movie director?" Sophie said.

"Sure," Mama said. "I think it sounds fun."

Sophie's thoughts swirled toward her like stars in hyperspace. She put her hand up to her forehead to slow them down.

"We don't have a video camera," she said. "I don't even know how to turn one on."

"That's where the deal comes in," Daddy said. He rubbed his hands together. "I will get you a camera—and I'll show you how to use it. Then you and Viola—"

"I think it's 'Fiona,'" Mama said.

"You two can create films with it if—and this is where your part of the deal comes in—"

I knew it, Sophie thought. She held her breath.

"If, starting with your next progress report, you have at least a C for the week in every subject. I know that you can do a lot better than that—"

"But it's a start," Mama said.

"That's our offer," he said. "What do you say, Soph?"

Daddy stood there then, arms folded, while Sophie fended off the shooting stars. The video camera had *huge* possibilities. But all C's? In less than two weeks? She felt so far behind already, there was no way she could catch up. Besides—she wasn't sure she knew *how* to make good grades.

"I don't know if I can *do* that," she said. "I'll *try*—"

"You're not stupid, Soph," Daddy said. "Anybody who can remember whole scenes of dialogue from a movie can retain enough facts to pass a sixth-grade history test."

"We'll help you any way we can," Mama said.

"That's a no-brainer." Daddy chuckled. "You have a scientist living right in your house. Science and math should be a snap for you with me around."

I hate science and math, Sophie wanted to say. *I hate school, period. And it hates me!*

"I guess I can try," she said.

"You're going to have to do more than try," Daddy said. "We'll have to see all C's on the next progress report." He pretended he was hitting a golf ball.

Antoinette moaned. There was yet another obstacle. But with a tilt of her brave French chin, she stiffened her lips and spoke aloud—

"Okay. It's a deal."

Six

It was raining the next morning—Tuesday—so Sophie went straight to the secret backstage place. She—and Antoinette—were wailing inside themselves.

"Antoinette! You look vexed."

Sophie squinted through the dusty dimness to find Fiona perched on top of a pile of old stage curtains.

"Does 'vexed' mean depressed?" Sophie said, climbing up beside her.

"More like distressed beyond words."

"Then I am."

"Uh-oh. Your psychiatrist was a total weirdo, right?"

Sophie shook her head so hard she stirred up dust in little gray clouds. "No! He was brilliant. He even said I shouldn't give up making up stories and pretending them."

Fiona's eyes widened. "So what's the problem?"

"It's totally heinous," Sophie said. And then she told Fiona all about the "deal."

"We could make *amazing* films—*brilliant* films," Fiona said.

"*If* I can pull a C in everything by *seven days* from now, which *isn't* going to happen."

"Why not? It's not like you're in classes for slow kids."

"I *should* be!" Sophie could feel tears threatening, but Fiona had a gleam in her gray eyes.

"What?" Sophie said.

"I'm an experienced tutor. Did it all the time in my old school."

"You could help me?" Sophie said.

"Hello?" Fiona's heart-shaped mouth formed a pink grin. "I'm your best friend, right?"

"But the teachers aren't going to let you sit next to me and help me the whole time. Especially Ms. Quelling."

"You mean Ms. Cruelling," Fiona said. "We'll just have to figure it out."

Fiona slid down from the pile of curtains, dug around in her backpack, and climbed back up with a spiral notebook with purple sparkles on the cover.

"This is my Idea Book," she said. She pulled a matching purple gel pen out of the spirals and folded the cover back with a professional air. "You miss stuff because you daydream in class, right?"

"Right," Sophie said, sagging again.

"So when you start drifting off, I'll make a signal—like smacking the desk."

Fiona demonstrated, raising dust from the pile of curtains. Sophie coughed.

"That's it!" Fiona said. "Coughing!"

"You mean, if you see me going off, you could just, like, clear your throat—"

"Brilliant!" Fiona said. "And then if that didn't get your attention, I could go on to a dry cough, like I had something in my throat."

"And if *that* didn't do it, you like bring up a hairball!"

By the time the bell rang, they had formulated an entire code.

Sophie managed to pay attention with an occasional hack from Fiona during language arts and social studies. In computer class, Ms. Yaconovich had made Sophie sit next to her desk since the first week of school, but Ms. Y wandered around the room a lot, pulling the Pops off the Internet.

Nothing bored Sophie more than moving paragraphs around, especially with what Fiona called mundane topics, like the amount of gold there was in Fort Knox.

But no matter how mundane, Antoinette had a job to do. And if her commanding officer wanted her to spy on the treasurer to preserve the colony's gold, then she must. The treasurer could be a Loyalist, and their precious savings could wind up in British hands. She peered into the tiny Treasury window.

A shadow fell across the beam of moonlight. Pulling her cloak around her, she ducked beneath the footbridge to avoid being seen.

"Your friend's got bronchitis or something," Maggie said.

Sophie saw Fiona doubled over, face purple and hacking from her chest in loud gasps.

"Oh no!" Sophie cried, and flung herself past three computers to reach Fiona's side.

"Fiona! Are you okay?"

"Yes!" Fiona hissed through her teeth. "I was using the code! I got all the way to Level Five!"

"Oops." Sophie whispered. "My bad."

"All right," Ms. Y said in her dry-as-sand voice. "Back on task."

Sophie took in a deep breath and went back to moving paragraphs around. She managed to get the assignment done before the bell rang.

"Could that have been any more boring?" she said to Fiona in the hall.

"Okay, forget it," Fiona said. "That scene is way over." She grabbed Sophie's arm and steered her toward the cafeteria. "I just had the most brilliant idea."

"For saving the militia?" Sophie said.

"This is better. Every time a new kind of video camera comes out, my dad buys it. We have like an entire attic full of old ones that still work. I bet he would just give one to you." Her eyes danced. "And *that* means you get your dad out of your face even *sooner.*"

"He will totally say no," Sophie said. "He always says no when it's me. When it's Lacie, he always says yes."

Fiona pursed her mouth into a rosebud. "Sophie, you have to stop being so pessimistic."

Sophie didn't even have to ask what *that* meant.

Antoinette rescued Henriette from a gold-filled pirate ship during free time after lunch. All through health, Sophie noticed Fiona's occasional "ahem" from her side of the room, but in math, Sophie never let her get past a Level Three bronchial spasm. By science, Fiona only had to fake pneumonia twice the whole class period. Sophie actually raised her hand to answer a question.

"That's the first day you haven't gone into a daze in my class," Mrs. Utley said after the last bell rang. She smiled as she spoke in a way that made all her soft chins wiggle. "Keep it up, Sophie, and you might actually move up to a D on your next progress report."

"Move *up* to a *D*?" Sophie wailed in the hall to Fiona. "My life is over!"

"She thinks it'll make you work harder, just to show her she's wrong."

"What if she isn't? What if I do get a D on my progress report? What if we don't get to play together ever again?"

"What if you stop thinking up that kind of stuff and concentrate on Antoinette? We have to make a movie!"

Sophie felt herself wilting. "Do you really think I can do this?"

"I don't think—I *know*," Fiona said. "I'll call you tonight, *mon amie*." She grinned. "That means 'my friend.'"

Sophie watched Fiona flit toward a black SUV. When Fiona opened the car door, the woman in the driver's seat chattered away in a foreign language to two little heads sticking up out of boosters in the middle seats.

Fiona popped her head out the window and yelled, "Call me as soon as you talk to your dad!"

But Sophie barely had a chance to say hello to Daddy when he walked in at suppertime just as the phone rang. It was a way-excited Fiona.

"He said yes!" she shouted into Sophie's ear.

"I don't know who that is," Lacie said, "but she doesn't need a telephone. Sophie, you have to help set the table. Get the knives and forks."

Sophie cradled the phone to her neck and pulled open the silverware drawer.

"Your dad said yes?" she said.

"He said to pick out any camera you want. We'll bring some over."

Sophie shoved the phone closer to her lips. "I haven't even asked my dad yet—"

Daddy looked up from a stack of mail. "What haven't you asked me?"

"My dad wants to talk to your dad," Fiona said. Sophie put her hand over the receiver and handed it to her father. He looked as if he had no *idea* what was going on.

But as she was dropping the last fork into place, Daddy hung up the phone and said to Mama, "Super nice guy. Very intelligent."

"Who?" Mama said.

"Viola's father," said Daddy.

"Fiona!" Sophie and her mom said together.

Daddy picked up Zeke just as he was about to poke his Spider-Man action figure into the spaghetti sauce bowl. "I'm going to *buy* a video camera from him, Soph. He's coming by next Saturday, *after* you've taken your tests."

"Does she still have to get a C in everything?" Lacie said.

"Is that your business?" Mama said.

"I still think you ought to make her go out for a sport," Lacie said.

"How about we sit down and ask the blessing?" Mama said. Zeke insisted they say the prayer four times because he had just learned it. Then Lacie snapped her napkin into her lap. "So some shrink says Sophie needs a video camera and she just gets one? Failing grades and all?"

"I'd watch that tone if I were you," Daddy said.

Lacie turned to Sophie and looked ready to explode right into the pasta. "I told you not to tell any of the other kids you were seeing a shrink!"

"It's nothing to be ashamed of," Mama said.

"True," Daddy said. "Although I don't think we need to be telling everybody our family business."

"This is going to get all the way up to the middle school, isn't it?" Lacie said.

"I only told Fiona," Sophie said.

"And she told her father, which means her mother probably knows—"

"I'm not even sure her mom speaks English," Sophie said.

Mama poised the salad tongs over the bowl. "Really?"

"She was talking some other language today in their car."

"Well, her dad speaks perfect English," Daddy said. "And I'm sure he has better things to do than spread gossip about Sophie, okay?"

Antoinette put her hands over her ears. Why did these noble people even listen to that little scullery maid? All she did was make trouble. Well, it wouldn't be long before saucy Lacette realized how Antoinette rose high above all such mundane things—

"Dream Girl," Mama said. "You need to eat."

Beside her, Lacie grunted and tore a piece of garlic bread in half. Sophie felt certain it was meant to be her.

Fiona and Sophie tried to pass the week until the next Saturday by concentrating on the first scene they were going to film when Sophie got her camera. *When*, not if. Sophie worked on homework with Fiona over the phone, and Fiona checked her work every morning—just in case Antoinette had taken over.

But every day on the playground after lunch, they launched into Antoinette and Henriette's stories no matter who might be around. And each time Fiona and Sophie climbed down from the monkey bars, Maggie lurked nearby. They made a pact to find out what she was up to.

On Thursday, just before end-of-the-week tests, Fiona and Sophie caught up to Maggie on their way to math. Maggie was walking in that very straight way she had, her head moving almost like a machine as she looked from side to side.

"Hi, Maggie," Sophie said.

Maggie turned to look at them. There was no expression in her eyes.

"You were watching us play, weren't you?" Fiona said.

"Do you have a problem with that?" Maggie asked.

"No!" Sophie said. The last thing she wanted was trouble. It wouldn't look good on her progress report.

"We just wondered," Fiona said.

Maggie hesitated, and then she nodded and fell in heavily beside them as they continued down the hall. "I mostly watch the other kids watching you," she said. "They think you're weird."

"So what else is new?" Fiona said.

"We're used to it," Sophie said. This felt so much easier with Fiona by her side.

"I know you guys make up stuff and play it," Maggie said. Her words thunked like tennis balls against a wall. "I like to play games like that too. Only I would never do it where these people could see me. You're just asking for it when you play make-believe out in the open."

"We're okay with it," Fiona said.

"We're not embarrassed at all," Sophie said.

"But you hate the teasing." Maggie said. "I know you do."

"They're just clueless Pops," Fiona said.

"I'm just telling you," Maggie said.

They walked the rest of the way to Mrs. Utley's room in silence. When they got to the door, Maggie said, "I'd play with you if you did it outside school. You don't play sports, so you're free after school."

"We have to get to class," Fiona said.

They hurried to their places. Sophie watched as Maggie sat at a table on the other side of the room.

"That's creepy," Fiona said. "It's like she's spying on us all the time."

It felt that way to Sophie too. And to Antoinette—

A cold chill crept up Antoinette's spine. Why did Magdalena lurk nearby always? Could she be a spy for her country? Was she after the gold as well? Perhaps she worked for the pirates. Antoinette glanced at Magdalena from behind her cloak. This girl would bear watching—careful watching.

"Ahem!"

Sophie looked at Fiona. "Good," she whispered. "You got it at Level One."

"Thanks," Sophie said. "What would I do without you?"

Sophie stuck out both of her pinky fingers. Fiona hesitated and then linked her own pinkies into Sophie's.

"That's our secret handshake," Sophie whispered.

On Friday morning, Fiona greeted Sophie on the stage with a frosted Pop-Tart.

"You can so do this," she said as she broke off a piece and stuck it into Sophie's mouth. "It's your mission."

Sophie felt her face soften with Antoinette thoughts.

"But don't go there," Fiona said. "Not until you get the camera. Tomorrow!"

"Progress reports don't come out till Monday," Sophie said.

"But you can find out your test grades today. Your dad's going to be so psyched; he might not wait till Monday. Come on—secret handshake."

That sealed it. Sophie marched into language arts and answered almost every question on the test. She knew the answers to all of them, but she didn't have time to fill in the last two.

"No worries," Fiona told her between classes. "You still probably got a C."

Social studies felt even easier. But when Antoinette began tickling herself with her quill pen, all Fiona had to hit was Level Two, and Sophie recovered. After their computer test, they practically danced to their chairs in the cafeteria. Maggie leaned across the table.

"Here comes Ms. Quelling," she hissed. "Don't look at her! She's mad."

"She's always mad," Fiona said, glancing up.

Sophie's heart froze when Ms. Quelling riveted her eyes first on Sophie and then on Fiona.

"I want you two in my room right now," she said. "We need to talk about *cheating*."

They followed her down the hall and into her classroom, their clammy hands clinging to each other.

"Sit," Ms. Quelling said. The girls sank into side-by-side chairs. Ms. Quelling picked up two papers. "How do you explain your almost identical answers on my test?" she asked, flicking her bright red nails like tiny daggers. "I thought you'd at least *dream up* an explanation."

Somehow Sophie found her voice. "I knew the answers, and I wrote them down."

"Suddenly you just *knew* the material after doing nothing in my class for six weeks?"

"I've been doing all my homework this week. And Fiona helped me study."

"That's right," Fiona said. "We studied a *lot* together." She pulled her bow-mouth into a line. "You think that's cheating?"

"*That* isn't cheating," Ms. Quelling said. "And I might even believe it, if someone hadn't reported to me that you have some kind of secret code going on."

"We do," Sophie said.

Ms. Quelling's eyes went round. "So you *did* cheat?"

"No!" Sophie said. "We don't use it to cheat. Fiona coughs at me when she sees me daydreaming."

"Everybody wants her to stop drifting off," Fiona said in a voice much pointier than Sophie's. "I'm just helping her."

Ms. Quelling laid the papers back on her desk. She looked disappointed.

"All right," she said. "I guess I don't have any choice but to believe that. I don't have any proof. But know this—I am going to be watching y'all *very* closely. Do I make myself clear?"

"Yes, ma'am," Sophie said before Fiona could say anything.

"Y'all go to class now," Ms. Quelling said. "Lunch is almost over."

Sophie bolted for the door, but Fiona lingered at the table.

"What is it?" Ms. Quelling said. Her voice stretched out like a rubber band. Fiona pointed to the test papers. "Could we please see our grades?"

Ms. Quelling made a loud click with her tongue. "They're both the same."

Fiona turned the papers over and grinned at Sophie. "B-plusses!"

"No way!" Sophie said. "I never made a B-plus my whole life!"

"Exactly my point," Ms. Quelling said. "Now go, both of you."

"I've been looking forward to seeing you again," said Dr. Peter as he ushered Sophie to their corner window seat that afternoon. "I want to hear more stories."

Sophie snatched up some hair. "I don't have any stories today. I'm sorry. If you're really disappointed, I can make up one right now."

Dr. Peter wrinkled his nose, but just a little. "I'm sure you could, but I'm curious. Why no stories today?"

"Antoinette would never have a problem like this," she said. "It's too heinous to even talk about."

Dr. Peter leaned forward. "Listen, Sophie: I will never tell anyone anything you say to me in here without your permission. What you tell me stays just between you and me."

"Would you put your hand on a Bible and say that?" Sophie said.

"I can do that," Dr. Peter said. "But I'd rather you just trust me."

Sophie squinted at him through her glasses.

"Do you even *have* a Bible in here?" she said.

"I couldn't help some of my clients if I didn't have the Bible."

"Oh," Sophie said. She took a deep breath. "Okay. Here's what happened." She told him all about Fiona and the deal with Daddy—and about Ms. Quelling and the cheating thing.

"If I have Ms. Quelling watching me every single second," Sophie told him, "and maybe the other teachers too, when she tells them—*which* she *will*—how am I supposed to focus? Already I only got a C-minus on my math test because I was so vexed!"

Dr. Peter tapped his lips with his thumbnail. "I understand you go to church and Sunday school every week."

"I do," Sophie said.

"So do I," he said. "Do you like it?"

Sophie took stock of her split ends. "Sometimes. But other times I daydream that it's Jesus up there preaching. That's okay, don't you think?"

"Absolutely," Dr. Peter said. "In fact, I was just going to suggest something along those lines."

"No, you weren't! Were you?"

"I wouldn't lie to you, Sophie," he said.

Sophie searched his face. There was no nose wrinkling or anything.

"I believe you," she said. "You seem very trustworthy."

"Here's my suggestion," Dr. Peter said. "As always, you can simply try it, and if it doesn't work, we'll try something else. But I think this is going to be perfect for you." He used his hands to explain in the air. "At home, when you're yourself and not Antoinette, I want you to picture Jesus, maybe the way you dream about him in church. And then I want you to talk to him about all these problems you're having."

"You mean out loud?" Sophie said.

"It doesn't have to be out loud. You can whisper, or you can just think it in your mind. Just be perfectly honest with him. You don't have to worry about what he thinks, because he already loves you totally. Just talk to him every day, even just for a few minutes."

"Am I supposed to imagine him answering me?" Sophie said.

Dr. Peter shook his head. "No. That's where it's different from your other daydreaming. You'll need to let him talk for himself."

Sophie could feel her eyes popping. "He's going to *answer* me? Like, out loud?"

"Probably not out loud like your father's voice or mine. Some people hear the Lord that way, but I personally don't."

"Then how?" Sophie said.

"I can't tell you exactly. You might feel something peaceful. Or you might not feel anything right away, but then later you'll realize something has changed. Sometimes Jesus gives silent answers."

Sophie pinched some of her hair between her nose and her upper lip and nodded. Dr. Peter pushed up his glasses.

"I don't think you're sold on this idea," he said. "But think about it and give it a try."

"One try?" Sophie said.

He twinkled a smile at her. "How about once a day until we meet next week?"

Sophie sighed. "All right," she said.

"One thing you can be sure of: he's going to listen."

That night as Sophie knelt by her bed to pray, she thought, *What if Lacie comes in and sees me and tells Mama and Daddy I'm playing Joan of Arc in here? What if Daddy thinks I'm double-weird? I never see* him *pray except in church and at the dinner table. What if I tell Fiona I'm doing this—and she doesn't want to be my friend anymore? I don't even know what religion she is.*

"Sophie?"

She jumped up and knocked her princess lamp against the headboard.

"You okay?" Daddy said through the door. "Sounds like the place is falling apart."

"I'm fine," Sophie said.

"Okay—lights out, then."

Sophie listened to Daddy's feet padding to Lacie's room.

"Come on in, Dad," she heard Lacie say. "Check out this game schedule."

Sophie shut her eyes. The kind face of Jesus smiled at her.

"Jesus," she whispered. "Does Daddy love Lacie more than he loves me? I should have told him and Mama about today, but I'm afraid. And Lacie always gets A's in citizenship. Lord, I don't want to feel like this. Amen."

But Sophie didn't feel peaceful. She just hoped that Dr. Peter was right.

Seven

Saturday dragged past breakfast and cartoons, past lunch and chores until the black SUV finally pulled into the driveway. Sophie hadn't had a minute alone to ask over the phone, but she hoped for the millionth time that Fiona hadn't told her parents about the cheating accusation.

But the minute she saw Fiona bolt out of the car, Sophie forgot about that.

Antoinette gathered up her skirts and rushed breathlessly to meet her friend. Although she knew it wasn't ladylike, Antoinette rushed past the woman climbing down from the carriage; so eager was she to get to Henriette.

"Whoa, there!" she said.

"Sophie—watch where you're going!" Daddy said.

"My word! Are you hurt?" said Mama.

Sophie snapped back to the real scene. A slender woman lay halfway on her back on the driveway. *That's not who picks up Fiona at school*, Sophie thought. Daddy pinched his eyebrows together as he grabbed the woman's hand.

"You need to be aware of your surroundings," he said to Sophie. "You knocked down—"

"Amy," said the woman, who rose to her feet. "Amy Bunting. And don't worry about it. I get tangled in those two almost daily." She nodded toward Fiona's little brother and sister who had climbed from the SUV and were already chasing Zeke.

A very tall man with bright eyes and narrow shoulders introduced himself as Ethan Bunting. When Fiona introduced Boppa, her grandfather, she planted a kiss on top of his bald head.

"Fiona talks about you all the time," he said to Sophie.

"Boppa, would you mind—?" said Mrs. Bunting. Boppa gave a here-we-go-again smile and headed toward the porch where Fiona's little brother and sister were climbing the railing with Zeke right behind them.

"I thought that other lady was your mom," Sophie whispered to Fiona.

"Marissa? No, she's our new nanny. Boppa loves to joke about how long she'll last. We've never had one stay longer than six months."

"How come your mom didn't go after them?" Sophie asked Fiona.

"She can save your life on an operating table, but she can't make those kids do anything. They're brats."

"Your mom's a doctor?"

"Yeah. She's a thoracic surgeon."

Sophie didn't ask her what *that* meant, but it sounded important and probably messy. Their dads stood at the back of the SUV, examining cameras. Fiona grabbed Sophie's hand and squeezed it as she dragged Sophie over there.

Daddy stood up straight just then, and Sophie's chest fluttered. He was holding a video camera.

"Is that it?" Fiona asked. "Is that the one?"

Daddy nodded, still peering at the camera with the ear-piece of his sunglasses in his mouth.

"Yes!" Fiona said. "Can we play with it now?" She reached to snag the camera.

She's going to get in so *much trouble*, Sophie thought.

But Mr. Bunting just said dryly, "You're so ladylike, Fiona." Daddy held the video camera out of Fiona's reach, his eyes glued to Sophie's.

"We saw our grades already," Fiona said. "She did great. Are you gonna make her wait till Monday?"

"Sophie knows when she can have the camera," he said, still staring straight into Sophie's eyes. "The Buntings have to leave shortly. They're on their way to Richmond for the week-end. I'll just hang onto it until we see that progress report Monday morning."

"Don't worry," Fiona whispered as her family loaded back into the car. "You *know* you're going to get it."

Antoinette did not appear for the rest of the weekend. But on Sunday night, Sophie grabbed her mobcap and stuck it on her head. She closed her eyes and tried to imagine Jesus.

"Is it ever going to be okay here?" she asked him. "Ever?"

Eight

As Sophie walked into school on Monday morning, she felt like throwing up her oatmeal. She imagined taking her progress report from class to class, her fate flowing from the tips of her teachers' pens as each signed off the form.

Antoinette pressed her hand to her stomach and tried not to think about the wretched gruel she'd eaten at the empty farmhouse. Lafayette's encampment lay before her, and she must now cross the James River without becoming seasick.

"Don't worry," Fiona said as they sat down in language arts. "We'll get seat work today so the teachers can fill out the progress reports—"

Anne-Stuart leaned across the table. "So, how do you think you'll do in here?" Willoughby leaned over Anne-Stuart's shoulder with a smile. They wore identical shirts.

"Are you talking to *me*?" Sophie said.

"I just wondered how you think you'll do on your progress report."

"I got a C on the test," Sophie said. "I didn't get to finish all the questions."

"Really?" Anne-Stuart said. She cocked her head, her head-band stretching her hair smoothly back from her forehead. "I thought you would do really well."

"You did?" Sophie said.

"You had plenty of help," Anne-Stuart said. "What did you get, Fiona?"

"A-minus." Fiona's nostrils flared like little trumpets.

"We studied together," Sophie said.

Anne-Stuart put a Kleenex to her mouth and coughed. Behind her, Willoughby coughed twice, and then yelped like a terrier.

"I don't get it," Anne-Stuart said to Fiona. She sniffed several times, and Sophie wondered why she didn't use the Kleenex for her *nose*. "How come Sophie got a C and you got an A-minus?"

"I don't know," Fiona said through her teeth.

Anne-Stuart coughed again into the Kleenex. Then Willoughby hacked like a cigarette smoker. Across the room came the sound of someone coughing up a lung. Sophie saw B.J. staring straight at her. Kitty cackled nearby, her ponytail flopping like a flounder.

Anne-Stuart stopped choking and leaned toward Sophie. "I guess a C is pretty good for you, huh?"

"Yes," Sophie said. "I'm trying to improve."

"Not that it's any of *your* business," Fiona said.

Anne-Stuart gave an innocent blink, her eyes sinus-watery, and coughed into her Kleenex. Willoughby choked and yelped as the last bell rang.

"All right, people," Mr. Denton said, his voice like a dial-tone. "I see only one person ready to work."

Sophie looked where he was pointing with his chin and saw Julia glance up from her open literature book as if she were surprised by the attention.

"She is so corny," Fiona whispered to Sophie.

Sophie pulled up the hood on her sweatshirt and stared at her open literature book without seeing a word.

At the end of the period, Mr. Denton laid the progress report in front of Sophie with a smile. There was a firm black C on it and the comment: *Much improvement! Sophie seems to be adjusting now.*

"We're on a roll!" Fiona said in the hallway. Sophie linked her arms in hers all the way into Ms. Quelling's room.

"I'm moving you, Sophie," Ms. Quelling said before Sophie could put down her backpack. "Over here where I *know* no one is going to help you." Ms. Quelling pointed to a seat right next to Julia and across from Anne-Stuart and Maggie.

"I trust y'all," Ms. Quelling said to them.

Julia and Anne-Stuart nodded solemnly at the teacher. Maggie offered one of her open stares, but the other girls didn't glance her way.

"That way you won't be tempted to even look at Fiona," said Ms. Quelling. "The assignment is on the board."

Anne-Stuart and Julia flipped their textbooks open.

"Aren't you going to get started?" Maggie said to Sophie.

Sophie tried to read about the writing of the Constitution and answer Ms. Quelling's questions. But she found herself writing things like *What if I still get a D because of my other tests?* so many times she almost wore down an entire eraser.

"Want one of my *new* pencils?" Anne-Stuart whispered.

"I'm fine," Sophie said.

"Sophie," Ms. Quelling said. "Look up the answers yourself."

But all Sophie could do was *pretend* to be reading. Even Antoinette could do no more than that.

The period dragged on until Sophie knew she would absolutely dissolve into a small puddle if Ms. Quelling didn't finish those reports in the next seven seconds.

And then suddenly Anne-Stuart whispered, "She's done!"

"You look scared," Julia said to Sophie.

Sophie didn't answer. She just watched as Ms. Quelling put a paper facedown in front of each student.

"If you've worked hard," Ms. Quelling said, "you have nothing to worry about."

No! Sophie wanted to cry out. *That's not true!*

Then Ms. Quelling put one at Sophie's place, and Sophie stared at its blank back.

What difference does it make? she thought. *Ms. Quelling hates me no matter what I do. I could get an A plus on my test, and she would probably still find a way to flunk me.*

Antoinette slumped in despair. With Henriette nowhere in sight, how could she find Lafayette here, trapped in the enemy camp? Where can I turn? she thought. And then it came to her, like a tiny candle flickering in the darkness. Go to the Master Jesus, it whispered. Imagine his presence. Antoinette raised her face to the light and closed her eyes. Behind her she heard a soft cough.

And then another, coming from Anne-Stuart. And still another, a louder one, from the back table, where B.J. was hacking into Kitty's sleeve.

"Do y'all need to go to the nurse's office?" Ms. Quelling said. "I'm going to start handing out cough drops at the door."

"You started it," Maggie said to Anne-Stuart, words thudding.

Both Julia and Anne-Stuart looked at her as if she were a passing worm, and then they focused on Sophie. She still hadn't turned hers over.

"The grade's on the other side," Maggie said.

"So—look at it," Anne-Stuart said. She crossed her fingers. "We're hoping for you."

Julia crossed her fingers on *both* hands and nodded toward the back of Sophie's paper.

Sophie wanted to fold it up and stick in her backpack and read it when there *weren't* three pairs of eyes watching her as if she were about to dive off a cliff.

But something stopped her. Maybe it was the crossed fingers and the nodding heads. Julia and Anne-Stuart could be rude sometimes, but who couldn't? Maybe they had some nice streaks in them, and maybe those were what were showing right now. Maybe they weren't more evil than good.

Slowly Sophie lifted the paper and looked at it. Julia and Anne-Stuart practically climbed across the table. Sophie saw the small B- in the space marked "This Week's Grade Average" and felt herself going limp.

"Is it bad?" Anne-Stuart said.

Sophie shook her head and turned it around. Julia's eyes scanned it and landed. Her smile stuck in place, but a storm seemed to pass over her face. Anne-Stuart gave Julia a stricken look.

Sophie pressed the paper to her chest. Neither of the Pops had said a word, but all traces of "We're hoping for you" were gone. She could only think one thing: *They were hoping all right—hoping I would fail.* An odd kind of nausea went up her throat. It had been one thing to be invisible to the Pops. But she was sure no one had ever *hoped* she would flunk. She shrank into Antoinette's cloak.

Maggie pointed at Sophie's paper. "What does the comment say?"

"I haven't read it," Sophie said.

"Well, look at it," Maggie said. "That's what *my* mother always goes for right away—the comment."

Sophie looked. *I'm seeing improvement*, Ms. Quelling had written, *but I suspect it hasn't happened honestly, though I have no proof at this time. Will watch the situation carefully. I have separated her from Fiona Bunting. Would advise that you do the same.*

"That isn't true," Maggie said over Sophie's shoulder. The bell rang. Sophie snatched up her backpack and charged for the door. Fiona was on her heels, and Sophie thrust the paper into her hands the minute they were in the hall.

"B minus!" Fiona said. "That's brilliant!"

"Read what she wrote, though!" Sophie said.

Fiona's eyes grew wider as they swept the page.

"No!" she said. Then she pushed the report back at Sophie and took out her own. "I haven't even read *my* comment," she said.

She pulled Sophie closer to her as they stared at Ms. Quelling's writing: *Fiona continues to do above average work. However, her recent association with Sophie LaCroix may hurt her. I suspect cheating and will continue to keep diligent watch. I trust you will take appropriate action regarding this new friendship.*

Fiona stuffed the paper into her pack like a wad of trash.

"That woman is beyond heinous," she said. "She's pure evil. And so are her little T.P.'s."

"T.P.'s?"

"Teacher's pets." Fiona's eyes went into little gray slits again. "Teacher's *Pops*."

Sophie felt a whisper of a smile on her lips. "You mean *Corn* Pops."

"They *are* Corn Pops!" Fiona let out a bitter laugh. "They're just corny and fake, but they think they're all that."

Sophie grinned. And then just as quickly, she felt the cloak fall on her, heavy and dark.

"What if our parents believe her?" she said.

Fiona shrugged. "Your parents know you're not a cheater." Fiona gave her a gentle push toward the computer room door.

"Let's get through this class so we can go play. I'm suffocating in this place."

The solid C in computers and Ms. Y's comment, *Good to see this*, didn't do much to lift Sophie's spirits. She was just surprised Ms. Y had managed to squeeze in a comment at all. Ms. Quelling had used up most of her space too, with her scissor-words.

Sophie said to Fiona when they were on the playground after lunch, "I'm sure Ms. Quelling hates me."

"It's not true."

They both looked down from the monkey bars. Maggie was squinting up at them, one sturdy hand shading her eyes like a salute.

"*What* isn't true?" Fiona said.

"That you cheated on the test in Ms. Quelling's class."

"No, it *isn't* true," Fiona said.

They both continued to look down at Maggie. Sophie didn't feel like talking to anyone except Fiona.

"Just so you know," Maggie said. "I know the truth."

She waited another few seconds, and then shrugged and walked away.

"I guess we weren't that nice to her," Sophie said. She threw her head down on her crossed arms. "I'm too depressed to even play."

In math Mrs. Utley gave Sophie a C- and wrote: *The grade is a gift for solid improvement. Expect to see more in the future.*

When she handed it to Sophie, Mrs. Utley said to both Fiona and Sophie, "Looks like you're having some problems in Ms. Quelling's class."

"It isn't true," Fiona said. "We don't cheat."

Mrs. Utley surveyed them from within the puffy folds around her eyes. "A little advice then?" she said. "Don't give anybody a reason to think you do cheat."

"Can I still help Sophie in this class?" Fiona said.

Mrs. Utley wiped her forehead with the side of her hand. "I'm going to let you, at least for the time being." And then to Sophie's surprise, she put her plump hand on Sophie's shoulder. "Just be sure you pay as much attention to *me* in class as you do to Fiona. Then maybe you won't need her help so much." She gave Sophie's shoulder a warm, damp squeeze. "You're a smart girl."

As the teacher moved slowly off to the next table, Kitty dropped a folded piece of paper in front of Sophie and skittered off.

"She's the Corn Pop errand girl," Fiona whispered. "Don't open it."

"What if it's an apology note?" Sophie whispered back.

"Are you insane?" Fiona said. Sophie slipped the note into her backpack. But she forgot about it the minute she climbed into the Suburban after school.

"How did your day turn out, Dream Girl?" Mama said. "Did you get your C's?"

Sophie nodded, although it was hard to even move her head.

"You don't seem very happy about it," Mama said. "This means you'll get your camera."

"Can I go to Dr. Peter today?" Sophie said.

"Not until tomorrow." Mama stopped at the stop sign and looked at Sophie. "All right now, you're scaring me. You look like you just lost your best friend."

"I think I'm going to!"

"Why?" Mama said. She pulled away from the stop sign.

Sophie took out the progress report and read Ms. Quelling's comment out loud. She could hear her voice trailing like a broken strand in a cobweb. Mama all but pulled over onto the side of the road.

"Sophie," she said. "What is going on? No, wait till we get home." Mama put her hand up and pressed the accelerator. She careened into the driveway like a NASCAR driver. Lacie bolted out the front door.

"Sophie's social studies teacher called," she said. "She wants you to bring Sophie straight back to the school—like NOW."

Nine

Sophie felt her heart slamming against her chest. *It's over*, she thought.

Everything is over. Mama didn't even get out of the car. "We have five minutes," she said to Sophie as the Suburban sent gravel flying. "So start talking."

As the neighborhood went by in a blur, Sophie told Mama everything. When they reached the school parking lot, Mama turned off the ignition and faced Sophie squarely across the seat.

"Look me in the eye," she said. "Did you and Fiona cheat?"

"No, ma'am," Sophie said.

"All right then," Mama said. "Let's get this mess straightened out."

Mama looked at least three inches taller as she marched up to the school. It made Sophie lift up her own chin and walk fast to keep up. Seeing Fiona in Ms. Quelling's room when they got there made her feel even stronger. Fiona was sitting calmly next to Boppa at a table, hands in her lap.

Boppa stood up until Mama had taken a seat. Ms. Quelling was nowhere around.

"Are you as fired up about this as I am?" Boppa murmured to Mama. He had a tiny red spot at the top of each cheekbone.

"I feel like a mother bear," Mama murmured back.

Fiona grabbed Sophie's hand under the table and held on.

It's all right, Antoinette tried to say with the squeeze of her hand. *Not even a council of Loyalists can take us down. We are the patriots in this battle. And we have the Wise Ones to defend us. We are not alone.*

The door from the hallway opened, and Ms. Quelling bustled in and opened her office door. Out came the train of Pops. Julia Cummings. Anne-Stuart Riggins. B.J. Schneider. Willoughby Wiley. Kitty Munford.

Fiona's hand gave Sophie's a clench that clearly said, *We're doomed.*

"May I ask who these ladies are?" Boppa said. He sounded proper, as if he were in a bank.

"These are the girls who informed me on Friday that Fiona and Sophie had a secret cheating code."

The Corn Pops all gazed innocently at Ms. Quelling. All but Kitty, who was swallowing as if she had an elephant stuck in her throat.

"And you believed them," Mama said.

"I listened to both sides," Ms. Quelling said.

"And you believed *them*," Mama said again.

Ms. Quelling wafted a hand over the Pops. "I've known all of them except Kitty since they were in kindergarten. They're nice girls." She cleared her throat. "However, I think it's possible that they were mistaken this time."

Julia's eyes startled, and she raised her hand halfway. "We aren't mistaken."

Anne-Stuart nodded. "We wouldn't have said anything if we weren't sure."

"I'm certain of that, girls. I just think someone else may have been privy to additional information." She tilted her chin toward the hall and called, "Come on in."

Maggie stepped in, stomping to the front like a chunky soldier.

"This is Maggie LaQuita," Ms. Quelling said to Mama and Boppa. "Maggie, please tell everyone what you told me."

"They didn't cheat," Maggie said. "Fiona and Sophie had a code of signals. But it isn't what you think. Fiona coughs at Sophie when she sees her daydreaming, so she can keep her mind on her work."

"How do you know that, Maggie?" Ms. Quelling said.

"I heard Sophie and Fiona talking about it all last week."

Julia raised an arm, ponytail swinging. "Maggie could be lying for them."

"I don't think so," Ms. Quelling said, her voice soft. "That's the same story Fiona and Sophie gave me Friday when I questioned them."

It sounded to Sophie as if Ms. Quelling were apologizing to the Pops.

"I'm sure you girls were just trying to help," Ms. Quelling said. "But next time, you might want to check out your facts a little better before you make an accusation, okay?"

"We never meant to make trouble," Julia said. Her friends all nodded except for Kitty, who put her face in her hands and cried.

"Did you want to say something, Kitty?" Ms. Quelling said.

"She's really sensitive," Anne-Stuart said. "She doesn't like to hurt anybody's feelings."

"None of us do," Julia said.

Fiona dug her nails so hard into Sophie's palm that Sophie was sure she was going to draw blood.

Ms. Quelling turned to the group at the table. "I'm sorry," she said. "I'm sure you can see why I was torn. I'll remove my comments from Sophie and Fiona's permanent records. Please accept my apologies."

"Apology accepted," Mama said without smiling. Boppa nodded in agreement. He didn't smile either.

"Can we go now?" Julia said.

"Yes. Thank you, girls," Ms. Quelling said.

The Corn Pops hurried through the door, and Maggie trailed out behind them. Fiona held onto Sophie for about fifteen seconds before they, too, escaped to the hall. By then, the Corn Pops were down at the other end, gathered in a circle around Kitty, who was wailing like a baby.

Maggie suddenly appeared and stood in front of Sophie and Fiona.

"Thanks for sticking up for us," Sophie said. "You saved our lives."

"Yeah, thanks," Fiona said. "Only from now on, could you not spy on us?"

"I won't have to anymore," Maggie said. "Because I'm going to be playing *with* you." She gave them a logical smile. "I figure now you owe me."

"Oh," Sophie said. "Well then, we'll see you tomorrow—at lunch, I guess."

As Maggie walked off in even, plodding steps, Fiona turned to Sophie, mouth already open in protest, but Boppa and Mama came out of Ms. Quelling's room.

"I'm sure you two want to spend some time with that camera tonight," Mama said. Her eyes were shiny. "Boppa says you can come over now and stay for supper, Fiona, if you both get your homework done first thing."

Fiona and Sophie squealed in unison.

After dinner, during which Sophie could barely take a bite of meatloaf, Daddy unrolled the progress report. He let his eyes work down to the bottom and rolled it back up. He tapped Sophie lightly on the head with it and gave her the Daddy-grin.

"Looks like I'm going to have to turn over that camera."

Sophie shrieked so loud she was sure she sounded like Willoughby.

Daddy showed them that the camera was pretty simple. The buttons he said she needed to know about seemed made for her as they fit in all their silvery-ness under her fingertips. The minute she squinted into the eyepiece it became *clear* that Sophie's world was meant to be seen through a camera lens. As she pointed it at Fiona, her friend filled a frame that shut out all the mundane stuff.

"Let's get started!" Fiona said to her. "Henriette and Antoinette are waiting!"

They worked until dark. When they viewed their first film on the camera's tiny screen, Antoinette and Henriette often had their heads chopped off, but Mama said it wasn't bad for a first try.

"We'll get better with practice," Fiona said.

"You think?" Sophie said.

"Oh, definitely. We can do this whole thing over tomorrow at recess."

Daddy looked up from the viewer. "You're talking about at school?"

"Yes," Fiona said. "We can do whatever we want after lunch for almost a half-hour."

"Sophie can't take the camera to school," Daddy said.

"Why?" Fiona said.

Sophie winced. Daddy looked startled that she had even asked, and his voice went into lecture mode. "One: it's expensive, and if it disappears, I can't replace it."

"My dad would just give you—"

"Two: I see nothing but trouble developing with those little—"

"Girls," Mama said quickly.

"—who can't mind their own business. And three: the whole idea of having this camera is to focus Sophie on her pretend stuff when it's appropriate. And that isn't at school."

Fiona watched him, bright-eyed. Daddy suddenly grinned at her. "Do you need more information?" he said.

"No, that's plenty," Fiona said.

"Why don't you two do your planning during free time and then do the actual filming after school and on weekends?" Mama said.

Fiona nodded. "We'll figure out a schedule." She looked at Sophie. "Do you have a planner on your computer?"

"I don't have my own computer," Sophie said.

Daddy groaned. "Don't put any ideas into her head, Fiona. The video camera about broke me."

"You're exaggerating," Mama said to him.

"He is the veritable master of hyperbole," Fiona said.

Mama and Daddy both stared at her.

"She has an excellent vocabulary," Sophie said.

"No kidding," Daddy said.

Even though the next morning was gray and misting, Sophie got up feeling lighter than she had since they had moved to Virginia. Fiona was waiting for her on the stage with two breakfast burritos, homemade by Marissa. Sophie smiled all through the morning. She even smiled at Anne-Stuart when she saw her in the hall outside Ms. Quelling's room.

Anne-Stuart sniffed at her. "Did you read my note from yesterday?"

"No," Sophie said.

Anne-Stuart whispered directly into her ear, "You should read it." She smiled in a wispy way and disappeared into the classroom.

"What did she say?" Fiona said. "Was it evil?"

"No," Sophie said. "She was being kind of nice."

Fiona narrowed her eyes. "Sophie, you trust people too much."

"I've just been thinking about it," Sophie said. "Julia said they weren't trying to get us in trouble. Maybe they thought they were doing the right thing."

"And maybe I'm Marie Antoinette and nobody knows it." Fiona leaned into Sophie. "Don't let them fool you. They're just manipulators. They turn things around any way they can to get what they want."

Sophie was quiet as she followed Fiona into the classroom. Why would the Corn Pops just decide they hated her and Fiona and want to get them into trouble? It didn't make any sense.

She reached inside her pack to get her textbook and remembered the note. She smoothed it out and she read Anne-Stuart's round, perfect handwriting, done in purple gel ink that smelled like grape bubble gum.

Dear Sophie,

I just want you and Fiona to know since your both new that me and Julia and B.J. have always been the top in our class. Just so you know what your deeling with.

Your friend,
Anne-Stuart

Sophie blinked when she got to the end of the note. *How did she get to the top of the class?* she thought. *She can't even spell, for one thing.* Still, Sophie felt stung. The Corn Pops had definitely *not* been trying to do the right thing.

She crumpled the note and stuffed it back into her pack, and she could almost feel the eyes boring into her from every direction. Sophie closed her eyes and imagined a quick glimpse of Jesus. He was smiling, kind as ever.

Okay, Sophie told herself. *As long as we're more good than evil, we'll always be all right.*

"Ms. Quelling—please!"

Sophie looked at B.J., who was leaning over Ms. Quelling's desk, raking her hand through her butter-blonde hair.

"If I do switch you with Maggie," Ms. Quelling said, "will you and Julia and Anne-Stuart yak your heads off?"

"No, ma'am," B.J. said. Sophie didn't see how B.J. could even talk with her lower lip hanging out that way.

"Why are you so hot on this, B.J.?" Ms. Quelling said.

B.J. squatted down and spoke so low, Sophie could barely hear her.

"I want to be moved away from Kitty," B.J. whispered.

Ms. Quelling nodded and gave Kitty a pointed look. "Fine," she said. "I'll switch you with Fiona."

"But I want—"

"How does it feel to want, B.J.? Work with me here."

Julia tossed her mane of auburn hair toward Anne-Stuart.

"It's okay," Anne-Stuart muttered to her. "At least she got away from Kitty."

Julia nodded. "We'll get us together again." She dug her eyes into Sophie.

Don't look at me, Sophie thought. *I didn't ask to sit here.*

As soon as they could get out of the cafeteria at lunchtime, Fiona and Sophie bolted for the playground. Fiona had her

Idea Book so they could plan how to redo their video. But no sooner had they settled themselves on the top bars than someone else climbed heavily up to join them.

"So what are we doing?" Maggie said.

Fiona pulled the Idea Book to her chest. "We?" she said.

"I get to play with you now, remember?"

"Oh, yeah," Fiona said.

Sophie's stomach churned. This was one kind of scene she didn't like—

Antoinette sighed and took Magdalena by the hands. "If you are to be one with us," she said kindly, "there are certain rules you must learn and follow. Can you do that?" Magdalena bent her head. "I would do anything to be a part of what you have with Henriette."

Sophie looked up sharply. Maggie was staring down at the hands that held hers. Sophie pulled her palms away. "You did practically save our lives. So—" She looked at Fiona. "Let's tell her our rules."

"You can't have rules," Maggie said. "There aren't any adults to enforce them. Can't we just get on with the movie? What about costumes?"

"We'll put them together," Fiona said. She was barely opening her mouth because her teeth were clenched together so tightly.

"You don't have to," Maggie said. "I have tons, and what I don't have my mom can make us. She's a professional tailor."

"Great," said Fiona. Her voice was as dull as Maggie's.

"You need me for something else too," Maggie said.

"What?" Fiona said between her teeth.

"Who's going to run the camera when you two are in a scene together?"

Fiona scratched at her nose. "You?"

"And who's going to play Lafayette?"

"You?" Sophie said.

Maggie shrugged. "So what are we waiting for? Let's get to work."

Ten

At free time on the playground and after school at Sophie's, the girls, including Maggie, practiced the rest of the week for Saturday filming. But there were problems.

In the hall after language arts class one day, B.J. "accidentally" ran into Sophie as she passed, shoving her into Fiona and landing both of them against the wall.

"Are you all right?" Anne-Stuart said. Fiona told Sophie later that Anne-Stuart's voice was laced with concern, but her eyes spelled pure contempt.

"What's contempt?" Sophie said.

"It's when somebody thinks they're better than you are," Fiona said. Fiona and Sophie weren't the only ones being tormented by the Corn Pops. Kitty Munford was now excluded from the Pops' lunch table.

But Kitty still trailed after them down the hall in spite of their curled-lip glares over their shoulders. She handed Julia and B.J. and Anne-Stuart notes, which they smelled and wrinkled their noses at and threw away. One day Sophie and Fiona even saw Kitty running after them on the playground wailing, "Why are you mad at me? Why don't you like me anymore?"

Julia finally stopped the whole group and turned around slowly to face Kitty.

"We're not mad," she said with a plastic smile. "We've just moved on."

Kitty covered her face with her hands and stood there sobbing as Julia led the Corn Pops away.

"That was just heinous," Sophie said to Fiona.

"But you know what's even worse?"

Sophie shook her head.

"Kitty still wants to be friends with them after the way they treat her. It's absolutely pathetic." Fiona pulled Sophie toward the monkey bars. "Come on. We have work to do."

And then, of course, there was Maggie. She was always armed with ideas she said were the *right* way to do things. It made Fiona talk with her teeth gritted.

But Maggie *was* teaching Sophie something new about the camera every day. Now when Sophie held it, her eye UNsquinted at the little window, she could turn it on with ease and zoom in or out on Lafayette or Henriette. She could imagine herself as a Hollywood director, hollering, "Cut!" and waving her arms to express how she wanted things done.

"Lafayette shouldn't just stand there," Fiona told Maggie one day when the three girls were practicing. "He was the commander of an *immense* army. He stood tall—"

"I thought you said he was short," Maggie said.

"But he could *look* tall," Fiona said through her teeth. "He was—*commanding.*"

You should know how to do that, Maggie, Sophie thought. *You command us all the time.*

The train of Corn Pops passed by just then.

"Flakes," Julia said to her followers.

Fiona watched them go by with contempt in her eyes.

"Flakes?" she said. "From a bunch of Corn Pops?"

Sophie felt a smile whispering across her face.

"What's so funny?" Maggie said.

"Well," Sophie said, "if they're the Corn Pops, then I guess we must be the Corn *Flakes*!"

"No way!" Maggie said. "I don't want to be a Corn Flake!"

But Fiona looked at Sophie and gave her husky laugh. "I love that!" she said. She reached out her hands to give Sophie the secret handshake.

"What are you doing?" Maggie said.

Fiona and Sophie looked at each other.

"It's just a thing we do," Fiona said.

"So—I'm a Corn Flake. I need to learn it."

"I thought you said you didn't want to be one."

Maggie looked at them soberly. "Maybe I do," she said.

With everything going on, Sophie now had to take more and more Jesus-breaks just to sit and feel his kind warmth. *If you love me*, she would think to him, *how come you don't make people understand me and my fellow Flakes?* There was still no answer, not one she could hear anyway.

But by Friday after school, Sophie could think only about their movie. She had scored B's on all her tests except math, which was a C+, and they were completely set for filming. They had chosen a wooded area near Poquoson City Hall as their setting. Mama said they were absolutely not going into some isolated area by themselves and arranged to go with them. Lacie pitched a fit, because that meant Mama wouldn't be at her soccer game, and Sophie held her breath until Mama said, "Don't start with me, Lacie."

At last, the mistress was scolding the maid Lacette. Antoinette tried to feel smug, but as she looked at Lacette's crestfallen countenance, she couldn't help feeling sorry for her, in spite of everything.

On Saturday morning, Sophie was helping Mama unpack the Suburban at the edge of the woods when Fiona arrived.

"I have a surprise," Fiona said. She held up a metal contraption with three legs.

"What is it?" Sophie said.

"It's a tripod. Boppa made it for us. There's a place to screw our camera to it so it won't wobble around so much. You can still pan from side to side and up and down if you want to, but it won't be all shaking from you or Maggie holding it." Just then a horn blew, and a faded blue car the size of a small boat pulled up. Maggie emerged from the passenger seat and motioned Sophie and Fiona to help retrieve three bulging garbage bags from the backseat.

Mama went around to the driver's side and stuck her hand in the window.

"I'm Lynda LaCroix," she said. "You must be Maggie's mom."

"I'm Rosa," said the older version of Maggie. For Sophie, there was just enough of a trill to her R to make her voice romantic.

"Sophie!" Fiona said. "Look at all this *cool* stuff!"

Sophie turned to where Maggie was pulling clothing out of a bag. She held up a pale pink satin dress with flounces on the sleeves and a lace-up front.

"This is yours," Maggie said to her. "There's a cloak in here for you too. Mom made it your size."

Sophie took the dress and held it against her as Maggie pulled out a long, forest-green dress with matching cape for Fiona and a dashing white uniform with red trim, for her to wear as Lafayette.

"That's exactly how I imagined him!" Sophie said.

"We looked it up in a book," Maggie said. "If we're gonna do this, we want it to be real, right?"

"Now all we need is a musket for him," Fiona said. She was breathless.

"I brought one," Maggie said. "It's fake, of course."

It wouldn't have surprised Sophie if it had been the real thing. Everything else was so *exactly* the way the guides in Williamsburg dressed that Sophie had to keep blinking to make sure she wasn't still dreaming.

Out of the last bag Maggie began to pull a black cape—velour, not velvet, but with a hood big enough for all of Sophie's hair. Its plush fabric never seemed to stop unfolding.

"Oh, Maggie," Sophie said. "It's magnificent!"

"I knew you'd say that," Maggie said. She didn't smile, but her eyes, for a moment, looked soft.

Breathless, Sophie donned the luscious black cloak. The woods were ablaze with autumn leaves. There was just a hint of a chill in the air. From someplace close by, someone had a wood fire going, so its time-honored aroma drifted into their scene. It was magically 1779 in Williamsburg.

With serious faces, Fiona and Maggie set up the tripod and made ready for the first scene. From then on, Sophie *was* Antoinette—elegant and brave and held in honor by Henriette and the Marquis de Lafayette. And yet she was also Sophie Rae LaCroix, famous filmmaker, intent on making a fine film that would pack theaters everywhere.

There were a couple of problems though. Once, Sophie forgot to turn the camera on, and they had to do a whole scene over. The other thing: Maggie couldn't act.

"She's like a stick saying words," Fiona whispered to Sophie.

Sophie tried to coach her, but Maggie just stared with a blank face.

"I wish you spoke French," Fiona said.

"I could do it in Spanish," Maggie said.

"Do that," Sophie said "At least it's a foreign language."

It helped. When they were wrapping up the final scene, Fiona said she wished they could go back and do *all* of Maggie's scenes in Spanish. It was already two o'clock, and they had to dig into sandwiches in the Suburban while Mama drove everybody back to their house to be picked up.

"I have an idea," Mama said.

"Is it scathingly brilliant?" Fiona said.

"I think so. Why don't we have a premiere at our house tonight?"

"What's a premiere?" Maggie said.

"It's a first showing," Fiona told her. "People get all dressed up—can we do that?"

"Absolutely you can," Mama said. "Soph, get Daddy to help you burn the DVD. And I'll set up the family room and make some *hors d'oeuvres*." Mama said they should invite their parents and come over about seven.

Sophie spent three hours getting ready, which was good because she wasn't allowed into the family room until Fiona arrived with Boppa.

"My parents already had plans," Fiona said. Her gray eyes were sparkling. "But your mom said I could sleep over."

When Maggie and her mom appeared, both with their hair up in fancy buns, Mama said, "Shall we go in?" She put out her hand to take Daddy's arm and led the way. Lacie wanted to know why she was wearing a long skirt just to go to the family room. Sophie swished her black cloak and wished Lacie would be whisked away by bats.

The family room was breathtaking, Sophie thought. Candles burning. Chairs set up like an intimate theatre. Computer-printed programs on each seat, announcing the premiere of *Antoinette and Henriette Save the Day for Lafayette.*

"This is fabulous," Mrs. LaQuita said.

"It's amazing," Daddy said. "My wife is terrified of the computer."

"You did a great job here," Boppa said.

Mama looked at Sophie and smiled her elfin smile. "It was worth it."

When the first scene finally wiggled its way onto the TV screen, Sophie was immediately lost in the delicious black cloak and the way it swirled when she walked. Lost in the drama of Antoinette begging Henriette not to die. She was even lost in the stiff-legged Lafayette, who looked into the camera when he was supposed to be professing his undying gratitude to Antoinette.

"Oops—there goes that fast pan again," Daddy said. He too seemed engrossed in their movie. "Who had the camera then?"

"That would be Sophie," Maggie said.

"You have to remember to move it very slowly, Soph," Daddy said. "Much slower than you would think. There are a couple of other things, but overall this isn't too bad."

"I think it's wonderful," Mama said. "Better than that thing we rented the other night."

Sophie wished everyone would simply watch the story. It was so beautiful she could hardly bear it. She could actually *see* what she had been dreaming of for so long, exactly the way she had imagined it. She had to put her hand to her chest so it wouldn't burst.

At the end, everyone clapped, and Boppa kissed each of the girls' hands. Maggie pulled hers away as if he had taken a bite out of it, but Sophie thought it was romantic. Everything was floating on a cloud—until Lacie ran out of the room choking and sputtering.

"She was laughing," Maggie said.

"What was your first clue?" Fiona said.

Sophie looked at Mama and Daddy, but neither of them went after Lacie to tell her how rude she was.

Let her laugh, Sophie thought. *Just wait until I become a famous movie director. Lacie won't scorn me then. That wasn't just a dream. It was really going to happen someday.*

Eleven

Late that night, with flashlights under the bedspread and the now dog-eared Idea Book, Fiona and Sophie got right to work on the sequel.

"You know something?" Fiona said. "Now that Lafayette has gone back to France, we don't really need him. We can write Maggie out."

"Wouldn't that be rude?"

Fiona pressed her mouth tight, and then she said, "I think she was the reason Lacie thought our movie was so lame. Maggie was always bossing us around. And then *she* couldn't act her way out of a wet paper bag. Wasn't it embarrassing to watch her play Lafayette?"

Sophie had to admit that it was. But she still had a squirmy feeling inside.

"We'll have to give back the costumes," she said.

"Oh, yeah—huh?"

"I really like that cloak."

"*You* make Antoinette what she is," Fiona said. "Not the cloak."

Sophie sighed. "We have to tell her in a nice way."

"I'm not as nice as you are," Fiona said. "You think of something."

Sophie closed her eyes. She imagined Jesus, although his eyes looked more sad than kind, and he wasn't smiling. When she imagined Antoinette, she was holding a feathered pen over a piece of parchment, but there were tears in her eyes.

"I think we should write her a farewell letter," Sophie said. "We should write like they did in the eighteenth century."

"Boppa has an actual inkwell—and those pens you dip in. He'll let us use that."

"Does Boppa say yes to everything?" Sophie said.

Fiona nodded. "He does it to make up for my parents, because they're never around." She tapped her Idea Book with her pen. "So—you dictate the letter to me, and then we can get all the stuff tomorrow and do the real one."

The letter Sophie came up with was, as Fiona called it, a masterpiece. It took them until longer than expected to get the eighteenth century version done, because Maggie showed up at Sophie's house Monday afternoon and wanted to know what the Corn Flakes were going to do next. They wouldn't be able to put the finishing touches on the letter until Tuesday, after Sophie's session with Dr. Peter.

"I don't see why you have to keep going to him," Fiona said. "You're doing so *good*! You're making B's now."

"I don't know," Sophie said. But she didn't really care.

The minute Sophie was curled up in Dr. Peter's window seat, she started right in. "Daddy still doesn't get me," she said.

"He's still after you about those daydreams, huh?"

Sophie hugged a face pillow to her chest. "It's better now that we're making them into movies. But it's still 'Sophie, do it this way.' Or worse, 'Sophie, why can't you be more like Lacie?' And he keeps reminding me that if I don't *keep* my grades up,

I can't use the camera. And I *have* to!" She tilted up her chin. "I'm going to be a film director someday. For real."

"I don't doubt it for a second," Dr. Peter said. "Would you like to try something fun with me?"

"Yes," Sophie said.

"I want you to pretend that you are *you*." He wrinkled his nose with a grin. "And I'll pretend to be your father. What's my name?"

"Daddy," Sophie said. "But couldn't it be like I'm Antoinette and you're my papa? Sometimes now when I don't know what to do, I imagine Antoinette, and then I know."

"Do you know why that is?" Dr. Peter said.

Sophie shook her head.

"Antoinette *is* you. She is the very strong and brave you. How do you think she got the way she is if *you* didn't make her up? She is the *you* who knows what to do."

"I don't get it."

"Let's try this and you be Sophie. Just say whatever Antoinette would say, and that'll be you."

"I'll try," Sophie said.

Dr. Peter sat up very tall on the seat and puffed out his chest.

"All right, Soph," he said in a deep voice. "Let's talk about those grades."

Sophie burst into giggles.

"Excuse me?" he said in a deep voice. "I'm not messing around here."

"You sound just like my father!" Sophie said.

"I *am* your father!"

"Okay." Sophie sat up straight on the pillows. "Father—oops—Daddy, I'm doing the very best work I can in school."

"Well, you're making B's now. But why can't you make A's? You're every bit as bright as your sister."

Sophie searched for Antoinette. "That may *be*—Daddy. But you know, don't you, that I'm not the least bit like Lacette."

Dr. Peter gave her Daddy's pinch between the eyebrows. "Who is Lacette?"

"Lacie! Daddy, we are not the same. And sometimes I feel as if, like, you want me to be her twin, and I'm not. I know I wasn't doing my best before, but now I am—and it's MY best."

Sophie realized that she was crying. She took off her salt-stained glasses. Dr. Peter handed her a Kleenex and waited for a moment.

"It's all right to cry," he said. "You're showing your true feelings, and that's what you need to do with your dad. Just the way you did it just now. You were very calm, very respectful."

Sophie shook her head. "He would still yell at me."

"How do you know that if you've never tried?" Dr. Peter wrinkled his nose. "You know what, Sophie? You have nothing to lose. You tell me he yells at you now, so what would be the difference? And he might not yell. He might be so surprised, he couldn't say anything at all."

Sophie giggled again. "Like *that's* ever going to happen. He can *always* say something. He's really smart."

"That's where you get your intelligence. And from your mom you get your creative side." He nodded. "God began a very good thing when he made you. I know he's very proud of you."

Sophie stiffened against the pillows. "I don't get that," she said.

"Get what?"

"If God—if Jesus loves me so much, then why doesn't he make people understand me?"

"Why don't you ask him? Are you still imagining him there with you?"

"Yes—but he doesn't ever *say* anything!"

"He's probably working in a different way. But I'll tell you something." Dr. Peter leaned forward like he was about to tell her a secret. Sophie found herself leaning in too. "You know how I said Antoinette knows what to do because she's in you?"

Sophie nodded.

"Jesus also shows you what to do because *he's* in you."

"He doesn't show me!"

"Sure he does." Dr. Peter laced his fingers around one knee. "I want you to try something else on your own — just for this week."

"I just have to try, right?" Sophie said.

"Yes, just try. Whenever you don't know what to do, instead of imagining Antoinette, I want you to imagine Jesus, just the way you've been doing. Ask him what to do." He grinned. "And then wait until you know that something is right, and then do it."

"Wait?" Sophie said. "What if one of the Corn Pops is in my face? I have to stop and imagine Jesus right then?"

Dr. Peter blinked. "You've lost me. Is this a new game — you being chased by cereal boxes?"

"Nooo!" Sophie explained the Corn Pops and the Corn Flakes to him.

"That's really clever," he said. "You know that, don't you?"

Sophie shrugged.

"Let me just say one thing about that, and then we have to finish up." He adjusted his glasses. "I think the names are great. Just be sure you look past the group's nickname. Be sure you look into each person. Especially when it comes to yourself."

"Okay," Sophie said.

"That's it for today then."

He high-fived her, and she was off to finish the letter with Fiona. When they were finished, there was only one tiny blob of ink on the paper, which Sophie thought made it more realistic. Still, when she and Fiona put it on Maggie's table first period on Wednesday, scrolled and tied with a ribbon, Sophie had a hard time letting go of it.

"It's going to hurt her feelings," Sophie said.

"Would you rather have her there bossing us around?" Fiona edged away from the table. "It just isn't the same with her there. I liked it better when it was just you and me."

Sophie at once felt sorry for Fiona—more sorry than she felt for Maggie. She left the parchment scroll on the table, and she forced herself not to look at Maggie the whole period. In social studies, Maggie wouldn't look at *her*.

"I think we worked it out," Fiona said after lunch. They were sitting on a set of swings no other sixth-grader would be caught dead on.

"I guess," Sophie said. "Did she read it? I didn't see her read it at all."

"I think we're about to find out." Fiona sat up straight. "Here she comes."

When Maggie reached the swings, Fiona said cheerfully, "Hi, Maggie."

"I didn't come to say hi," Maggie said. "I came to say that you didn't have to go to so much trouble because I thought the movie was stupid anyway." She gave her dark hair a flip with her hand. "And who *wants* to be a Corn Flake?" Then she turned and walked back toward the school building.

"She thinks she's 'all that,'" Fiona said.

Sophie pulled a strand of hair under her nose. "I don't want to talk about it right now." She closed her eyes and imagined Jesus. He was as kind as ever. She felt worse.

What do I do? Sophie said to him. *I don't think what we just did was right—but I don't know what to do. If I call Maggie back,*

Fiona will be mad at me. She probably won't want to be my friend anymore.

She waited, just as Dr. Peter had told her to, but there was no sudden burst of inspiration. There was only Fiona saying, "Come on—that was the bell."

Sophie climbed off the swing, but Fiona stayed on hers.

"Soph?" she said. "Are you mad at me?"

"No!" Sophie said.

They gave each other weak smiles and walked back to the building together.

But for the rest of the day, Sophie felt more alone than she had in a long time. The office lady bringing her a note last period from Mama didn't even help: *Your mother is going to be about ten minutes late picking you up. She wants you to wait on the playground, and she will find you.*

"They must have told her in the office that's the safest place to be after school," Fiona said. "There's always a teacher out there." Fiona tilted her head almost shyly. "I wish I could stay with you."

Sophie said she wished she could too, but secretly she was glad to be alone as she headed for the swings. She needed to badger Jesus until he showed her something. Sophie pulled up her sweatshirt hood. The thought of her lost black cloak stabbed her.

"Jesus?" she whispered. "Did we do the wrong thing, kicking Maggie out?"

There was a scream—though Sophie knew right away that it wasn't Jesus answering her. It was coming from across the playground, where a small group was streaming away from the fence, leaving behind a lone figure who was waving her hands and screaming. It was Kitty.

The group walking away from her was the Corn Pops. Not a single one of them looked back.

Sophie took off toward Kitty, but Julia planted her tall self right in Sophie's path.

"Don't go there," Julia hissed. "Just leave it alone, or you are going to be so sorry."

Twelve

✿ ⌂ ❂

Julia kept looking at Sophie through hardened eyes — until Willoughby gave a stifled squeal and B.J. pulled at Julia's elbow.

"Mr. Denton is coming!" she said in a hoarse whisper.

"Just leave it alone," Julia said to Sophie one more time. Then she was gone, with her train of Pops behind her.

Do they really think Mr. Denton isn't going to see Kitty over there freaking out? Sophie thought.

"Everything all right out here?" Mr. Denton called.

"Yes!" Kitty called back. "I'm fine!"

Mr. Denton waved and sat down on a bench by the door. Sophie hurried over to Kitty and squatted down beside her.

"Why did you tell him you're fine?" Sophie whispered to her. "What did they do to you?"

Kitty's face was smudged with dirt on both cheeks, except where tears had left their trails on the way down her face.

"Please don't tell anybody," she whispered. "Please."

"But *why*?"

"Because!" Kitty rubbed her eyes with the backs of her hands, leaving them smeared with dirt.

Sophie grabbed one of Kitty's dirty hands. "What happened?"

"You have to promise you won't tell anybody else — and you can't tell Julia and them that I told you either."

Kitty hung her head until all Sophie could see was the top of her ponytail. "I had to crawl on the ground. They told me that if I crawled across the playground on my hands and knees, they would take me back into their group."

"What?"

"And then after I did it, they laughed and said they were only joking. They never wanted me back in their group at all!"

Kitty shook her head so hard, Sophie was afraid she was going to break her neck.

"Stop!" Sophie said. "They aren't even worth it! They're just — cruel. They're evil — they're heinous!"

A whistle echoed across the playground. Sophie whirled around — but it was only Mr. Denton. Mama was standing next to him with Zeke, waving at her.

"I'm coming!" Sophie called to her. She turned back to Kitty.

"Please don't tell anybody," Kitty said. Her eyes were pleading. "If you do, they'll find out about it — they know *everything* — and they'll do worse to me."

Sophie didn't know what to say, and Dr. Peter had told her to wait if she didn't know.

When she got home, Sophie went straight to her room. Her stomach was tying itself into a knot as she sat cross-legged on the bed.

"Jesus?" she whispered. "I saw two people get really hurt today. I think I have to do something about it. I'm just going to ask you what to do, and then I'm going to wait until I know. Because somebody has to do something. And I think it's supposed to be me. Is that why I'm feeling so sick?" She swallowed hard. "Or is it because I was hurting somebody else myself?"

Sophie kept her eyes closed and waited. Just as always, there was no answer she could hear from Jesus. She wiped her wet face. "It's *wrong*," she whispered.

After she somehow got through dinner, Sophie called Fiona.

"There's something we have to do," Sophie said when she had Fiona on the line. "But you have to promise not to tell a single other person, or Kitty is going down."

"Kitty?" Fiona said. "Do we care about Kitty?"

"Yes," Sophie said. "We do."

Sophie told Fiona everything she had witnessed on the playground.

"So what are you saying we should do?" said Fiona.

"I think we should rescue Kitty."

"What?"

"And I thought about something else," Sophie said. "What the Corn Pops did to Kitty is no different from what we did to Maggie."

"It wasn't like we just stopped being her friends! We were *never* her friends!" Fiona's voice was winding up. "She pushed herself right on us. She was making us pay her back for something she did for us, and we paid her back. We're done."

"I just don't like the way we did it," Sophie said.

"It was *your* idea!"

"I know. And that's why I think we should tell her why we got mad at her and give her one more chance."

"No," Fiona said. "And you know what else? I'm not helping Kitty either. Has she ever once been nice to us?"

"I don't think that makes any difference," Sophie said. "We should do the right thing."

"*You* do the 'right thing,'" Fiona said. "Not me!"

Suddenly there was a click in Sophie's ear. Fiona had hung up.

Sophie flung the phone onto its cradle and climbed the stairs in a blur. But when she tossed her glasses onto the bedside table and threw herself face down on her bed, her chest was pulled in so tightly she couldn't cry. She could only lie there with hurt all around her until a knock sounded at her door.

"It's seven thirty," Daddy said. "You only have an hour and a half before lights out. Did you get your homework done?"

She really wished he would go away. She was afraid she was going to either throw up or cry, and she would have to explain either one. Dr. Peter had told her Daddy might understand if she just talked to him calmly—but now just wasn't the time to try that.

"I'm about to, Daddy."

"Okay. Well, let's get it done." Daddy opened the door a crack. "You want to keep that camera, right?"

Sophie nodded.

"Now that you're on track, I want to see some steady improvement. Let's make that the rule starting next week."

He ran his hand over her hair and left, whistling. Sophie felt as if a steamroller had just knocked her down. She couldn't do her homework. She couldn't even think about how she was going to rescue Kitty all by herself, or even how she was going to apologize to Maggie.

All she could think about was never being friends with Fiona again. Never having lunch together, never meeting on the stage behind the curtains with homemade breakfast burritos, never hanging out on the monkey bars and planning brilliant films.

She finally snapped off the light and crawled under the covers. *Is everything going to go back to the way it was before*

Fiona? she asked Jesus. *If you love me, why would you let that happen? Help me get her back, please.*

Just one more thing, she said to the kind-eyed man in her mind. *I won't crawl in the dirt for Fiona, okay? Please don't let her ask me to do that.*

And then she started to cry.

The next morning, being-scared nausea swept over Sophie as she walked through the school hallway alone.

What am I supposed to do now? she thought. *Fiona isn't waiting for me backstage. I can't go there by myself.* She put her hand to her mouth. *I wouldn't be able to bear it!*

Instead, she turned toward the language arts room. Maybe Mr. Denton would let her come inside and sit. Although what she was going to do or think about or dream up, even she couldn't imagine.

Sophie hadn't taken more than two steps when a skinny figure was beside her, sniffling.

"You've been crying," Anne-Stuart said in her clogged-up voice.

Sophie tried to ignore her and set her sights on Mr. Denton's door.

"Is it about Fiona?" she said. "She's been crying too. Julia's trying to help."

Anne-Stuart pointed a shiny-nailed finger. Sophie nearly tripped on the carpet. Fiona was against the wall, across from the language arts room, and Willoughby and B.J. stood in front of her, leaning in as if Fiona were giving them the ultimate secret to popularity. But it was Julia who astounded Sophie the most. She was standing next to Fiona—*with her arm around her.* And Fiona wasn't even flinching.

Thirteen

Sophie pushed open Mr. Denton's door and made her way to her table. She sank down into her chair, her backpack thudding the floor beside her. She put her head on her arms and tried to let Antoinette take over and push away the heinous sight of Fiona joining the Corn Pops.

Antoinette sat down beside her and pulled the black velvet cloak around both of them. "I'm so sorry, my gentle friend," she said, *"but I am not your answer. The good doctor, the* brilliant *doctor—he gave you the answer. You must follow that now."*

Sophie squeezed her eyes tighter. *You're leaving me too, Antoinette? NO—come back!* But Antoinette didn't, and Sophie felt more alone than she ever had. Maybe if she called Mama and told her she was really in trouble, they could go to Dr. Peter right this minute. He could tell her what to do. And then Sophie knew something: he already had told her what to do. With her eyes squeezed shut against the hot tears, she prayed.

The kind face was there in her mind—the Jesus face she always imagined. Not Antoinette's face. Not Fiona's face. Just Jesus'. And he had already shown her what to do. *If I have to do it on my own—then please will you help me?*

The bell rang, jangling her face up from her arms. The room filled with jabbering students followed by a substitute teacher. Sophie couldn't look to see whether Fiona would sit with the Corn Pops. Instead, she looked for Maggie.

I have to tell her I'm sorry, Sophie thought. She didn't know anything else at the moment, but she knew that.

As Sophie watched, Maggie settled herself into a corner and opened a book. Sophie glanced around and realized that on the board the sub had written: *THIS IS A FREE READING DAY.*

This is my chance, Sophie thought. *But what if I apologize and Maggie just yells at me?* And then she could almost hear Dr. Peter in her head: *She gets in your face anyway. What have you got to lose if you talk calmly and honestly to her? You'll never know unless you try.* Sophie wove her way through people who *weren't* reading. Maggie slammed her book shut just as Sophie sat down next to her.

"Hi," Sophie said. "What are you reading?"

"What do you care?" Maggie said.

Sophie squeezed her hands together. "I do care. Fiona and me, we made a huge—an *immense*—mistake when we wrote you that heinous letter. I hope you'll forgive me."

"Are you ever for real?" Maggie said. "Or is everything a big act to you?"

"This *is* real," Sophie said. "We thought you were *way* bossy when we were making our film, and we didn't like it. But we should have told you the truth." She had to stop and take a deep breath. "I want you to be a Corn Flake again, and I'll even help you remember not to be pushy. We can do the secret handshake—and we have a very important film to do. This one—"

But she stopped, because Maggie was shaking her head.

"Why not?" Sophie said.

111

"Because you just want the costumes," Maggie said. "My mother thinks you just used me, and she said if I start being friends with you again she'll ground me. Face it: Fiona dumped you and joined the Corn Pops, so now you need a friend." Maggie opened her book again. "It isn't going to be me," she said, and then she glued her eyes to the page and shut Sophie out.

But not before Sophie saw the title on the cover: *The Story of the Marquis de Lafayette.*

She wants to be friends—I know she does, Sophie thought as she moved back to her table, her feet like a pair of concrete buckets. *But we hurt her feelings so bad that even her mom hates us now.*

Suddenly Sophie knew something else too. Once you hurt somebody, you have to take the consequences. She looked over at Kitty, her literature book open and her eyes wistfully watching the people who had made her crawl across the playground like a dog.

I want the Corn Pops to know that too, Sophie thought. *I have to find a way. Even if I have to do it alone.*

As soon as she could at lunchtime, Sophie fled from the building. She couldn't bear to go to the monkey bars. *It's bad enough that Fiona doesn't want to be with me,* she thought miserably. *But I never, ever thought she would be a Corn Pop.*

But she had a mission. Sophie plopped into a swing and pored over her social studies book to find out what Lafayette and George Washington had done in their rescue of America. It wasn't *exactly* the same thing, although she found some inspiring ideas—like the patriots digging trenches called "redoubts" to hide in and trapping the British "handsomely in a pudding bag."

Sophie closed her eyes several times and imagined Jesus when the planning got too lonely. He was always looking at her with kind eyes, but sad ones too—as if he understood that even though what she was doing was right, he knew it wasn't fun for her without Fiona. *I'll just have to go back to pretending on this plan*, Sophie said to him in a prayer. Daddy wouldn't like it, but she couldn't help thinking Jesus did.

This plan just might work. It had to.

After school, Sophie couldn't wait to get to Dr. Peter's window seat.

"Sophie-lophie-loodle!" he sang out. "I can tell you've got something on your mind today." Dr. Peter was barely seated before she was pouring out the whole Maggie and Kitty and Fiona story. Dr. Peter listened and nodded. There was no twinkle at all.

"Can I just tell you how proud I am of you?" he said.

"I feel wretched," Sophie said.

"Well, look at you. You went to Jesus. You asked what to do. You waited. He showed you—and you did it."

Sophie shook her head.

"No?" Dr. Peter said.

"Yes. But I'm still not sure *how* he showed me. I want to know in case he does it again."

Dr. Peter spread out his fingers and counted on them as he talked. "Showing number one: you never go out on the playground after school, but the day you did, there were the Corn Pops giving Kitty the worst time ever. Didn't that turn you around completely?"

Sophie nodded.

Dr. Peter started on another finger. "Your prayer showed you later that you had to get with Fiona and apologize to Maggie.

None of that has worked out the way you want—yet. But you did the right thing. And besides that—" His eyes twinkled as he went to finger number three. "You had a substitute so you could talk to Maggie."

"But what *about* Maggie?" Sophie said. "She still hates me."

"I think Maggie is still choosing. Otherwise, why the continued interest in Lafayette? Just because *you* take the opportunity Jesus gives you doesn't mean everybody does. You can't decide for another person. You can only give them the chance."

"So—let me get this straight," she said.

"Okay." Dr. Peter wiggled all his fingers, telling her to bring it on.

"When Jesus 'shows' me something, it isn't like *boom*—there it is! It's more like he gives me an opportunity, and then I decide whether to take it or not."

"Exactly," Dr. Peter said. "That's how it works."

Sophie tickled her nose with her hair. "But what I still don't get is, if Jesus loves me so much—"

"Okay, there's your hang-up," Dr. Peter said.

"Where?"

"That 'if.' When you say '*If* God loves me—*if* Jesus loves me,' that means you have some doubt. As long as you have that 'if,' you're going to doubt the opportunities that Jesus puts right in front of you. I'm sure that bums him out." Dr. Peter leaned forward. "God loves you. There is no 'if,' Loodle. That's why he sent Jesus to show us the way—he loves you *that* much. He's our Father—and you know how much a father loves his kids."

Sophie looked down at the ends of her hair.

"What?" Dr. Peter said. "You don't think your father loves you?"

"I know he loves me," Sophie said. "But I don't think he loves me *that* way."

"Tell me some more."

"He would love me more if I did even better in school," she said slowly. "And if I played sports and joined all these clubs. I do think he loves me more than he did when we moved here. But it's never going to be enough, because—"

Dr. Peter's voice went down to an almost whisper. "Why, Sophie?"

Sophie squeezed her eyes shut tight. "Can I tell you something I've never told anybody else in the entire galaxy?"

"If you want to."

"I think my father loves Lacie more than he loves me."

"Sophie," Dr. Peter said, "do you remember when I told you that I would never tell anyone anything you said in here without asking your permission?"

Sophie nodded.

"I'm asking permission now to share this with your father."

"But he'll get mad at me!"

Dr. Peter smiled at her. "We'll never know that, will we, unless we try." Dr. Peter said there was one more thing.

"The key to everything is knowing that God loves you, and he shows you that love through Jesus. If you really want to believe that, you need to get to know Jesus better—not just in your imagination, but from who he is." He rubbed his hands together. "How did you learn more about Lafayette so you could start a good Kitty Rescue Plan?"

"From our social studies book," Sophie said.

"Okay—God has a book too."

"The Bible."

"Brilliant! Next time, we'll start reading the Bible and getting to know Jesus' plans too. But for now, you just focus on your plan to rescue Kitty." He stood up and grinned at her.

"I know this is hard, Sophie-lophie, but you go for it. I'm so proud of you."

That—and her talks to Jesus—carried Sophie through another evening without a phone call from Fiona. In fact, the next morning as she stepped inside the school building, she was ready for Scene One.

Kitty sat on a bench, looking painfully alone, staring at the literature book that Sophie could tell she wasn't reading. On the other side of the hall, the Corn Pops were standing in front of the trophy case, comparing new sweaters with their backs very deliberately to Kitty. At least Fiona wasn't with them.

Sophie headed straight for Kitty. "Come with me, would you?" she whispered to her.

Getting her away was like peeling a sticker off a mirror, but Sophie managed to drag her through the double doors and into the hall in front of the office where nobody hung out. By then Kitty was barely breathing.

"You didn't tell anybody, did you?" she said. "I told you not to tell!"

"It's not about that," Sophie said. "I just want to tell *you* something." She took Kitty's hand, Antoinette-style. "Those girls out there—you don't need them. They're mean to you."

Kitty whimpered. "I know. But I'm so mixed up!"

"Why?"

Kitty pulled in air that sounded ragged. "I knew they could be sort of mean. Like when they got jealous of you and Fiona doing good in class, they *looked* for ways to get you in trouble. Like they swore you made up the coughing code so you could cheat, even though they didn't know for sure. I got really scared then about saying stuff about people that wasn't exactly true, and that's when they decided to dump me." Kitty shuddered. "Then I saw how mean they can *really* be, and I

116

just want them to leave me alone now. Only—" She put her hand over her mouth and mumbled into it. "I just don't want to be all by myself."

"You don't have to be alone," Sophie said. "They're not the only girls in the galaxy. You can be my friend."

Kitty looked at her, and then darted her eyes away. "No offense," she said. "You're really nice, but I want to be with the popular girls. I was way popular at my last school. Now I don't know if I'll ever be popular again."

"You don't have to be popular to have fun," Sophie said. "I have a *lot* of fun when I'm with—well, I have fun."

Kitty didn't look at her this time. "But everybody thinks you—and Fiona—are weird." She burst into tears. "I don't want to be weird!"

Sophie knew that at this point Fiona would be telling Kitty that *she* was the one who was weird. Sophie actually considered it too, but instead she said, "There are four other girls in our class besides us and the Pops—"

"They're the soccer players. I can't—"

"Okay. Well," Sophie said, "if you ever decide you don't mind being with weird people, come see me, and I'll be your friend. But in the meantime, I can still help stop Julia and those other girls from being mean to you. It won't make them be friends with you, but at least they'll leave you alone."

Kitty shook her ponytail sadly. "Nobody can stop them, because everybody thinks they're wonderful. I told you, even the teachers wouldn't believe me."

"They would if they *saw* them being mean to you."

"Unh-uh. They never do anything mean when teachers are watching."

"Leave that to me," Sophie said. "Just come out to the playground after school."

"But that's when they do mean stuff to me!" Kitty said. "They know the teacher on duty doesn't get out there until way after the bell."

"Trust me," Sophie said. "Please. All you have to do is, when they start to do something to you, *run* over to where I'm playing. They'll follow you, and I'll do the rest. Mr. Denton will have seen what he needs to see already. I promise you."

"I don't know," Kitty said. "I can't even stand it when they *start* with me!"

Kitty bolted for the girls' restroom. Sophie watched her for a minute and then trudged the hall to the language arts room. She could almost hear Dr. Peter saying, "You've given her an opportunity. Now it's her choice."

Fourteen

Scene Two didn't go the way Sophie hoped it would either. She went up to Mr. Denton at the end of language arts and asked him if he could come out to the playground *right* after school.

"As soon as the bell rings, if that's feasible," she said.

"Actually, I'm not on duty today," he said. He folded his arms and smiled, something he didn't do very often. "Too bad too. You've got me intrigued."

Sophie squinted her eyes. "Who *is* on duty today? Mrs. Utley?"

Mr. Denton shook his head. "Ms. Quelling is the victim today."

"Oh," Sophie said.

She could feel herself wilting as she turned away.

"Something I can help you with?"

Sophie looked at Mr. Denton in surprise. He was giving her a kind look. That was why she said, "Do you pray?"

"I've been known to," he said.

"Then please pray for me today. I need it."

"You are a fascinating child, Sophie LaCroix," Mr. Denton said. "You have my prayers."

Sophie felt a little better after that, especially as Scene Three of the plan unfolded. Out on the playground after lunch, she was able to dig a trench—her "redoubt."

I think the actual ditches the soldiers dug were deeper than this, Sophie thought as she worked. But she really didn't want anybody to break a leg. She disguised the trench with some branches and then gave a big sigh. This would have been brilliant with Fiona. There would have been so much more to it—they were such a good team.

"*Were*," Sophie said to herself.

Before she could start crying, she headed back toward the school building. Near the back door, the Corn Pops were all gathered, watching Anne-Stuart French braid Julia's hair. Fiona was nowhere to be seen. They stopped their conversation and put on identical freeze-dried smiles as Sophie started to pass.

"Hey," Julia said.

Sophie had to look twice to realize Julia was talking to her.

"Hey," Sophie said back. She edged toward the door.

"Are you trying to be friends with Kitty now?" Julia said.

Sophie took a deep breath. Fiona always handled this kind of stuff.

"Does it matter to you?" Sophie said. "You're not friends with her anymore."

"No," Anne-Stuart said. "But—well—" She looked at the rest of the Corn Pops, and they all nodded as if they already knew what she was going to say. "I don't mean to be talking bad about Kitty," she went on, "but she whines *all* the time. She always makes everything look worse than it is because she *cries* so much."

"I wonder why?" Sophie said. She knew that her pipsqueak voice didn't make her sound sarcastic the way Fiona could.

"So," Julia said, "are you going to be friends with Kitty now?"

"If she wants to be," Sophie said. "I asked her to come out and play with me today after school."

"Really?" Anne-Stuart said. "Is she coming?"

Sophie didn't answer. She was too busy asking Jesus to forgive her if she was pulling Kitty into a trap. But this had to be part of the plan—and the Corn Pops had just made it so easy.

Julia patted her newly braided hair. "It's nice to know she'll have someone to *play* with, since we don't *play*." She lowered her voice as if to include Sophie in a little-known fact. "Just be careful. She really is a whiner."

"Yeah," Willoughby said, in her usual whine. "We hate that."

Scene Three closed as the bell rang, and Sophie waited until the Corn Pops were inside before she fell into the line filing through the door.

I think they'll be there, she thought. *Because they don't want Kitty to have any friends. Or me either.* It gave her a chill that went all the way to her backbone.

Kitty was hanging just inside the door when Sophie got there. Her freckled face was a tangle of confusion.

"I saw you talking to them," she whispered to Sophie.

"I was setting it up," Sophie whispered back. "You have to just trust me."

As Sophie continued down the hall, she heard Kitty whimper.

I wouldn't blame her if she never trusted anybody ever again, Sophie thought.

Just as soon as the bell rang at the end of the school day, Sophie went into high gear to get ready for Scene Four.

She raced to the bathroom and got into costume. The old bedspread from the attic wasn't one tenth as wonderful as the cloak Maggie's mother had made for her, but Sophie decided she would just have to be a better actress to make it work—although it was going to be hard enough doing the scene all by herself.

It doesn't have to be good, she told herself. *It just has to do the job.*

She looked at her somewhat ragged self in the mirror. *I'm Antoinette, and I'm tattered from this long war. But I'm ready to face the British so the final battle can begin!*

When she got to her spot by the fence, Sophie cleared off the branches and lay down on the ground, looking over the top of the redoubt. All she could do now was wait for Kitty and the Corn Pops—and hope Ms. Quelling had shown up for duty.

Why does it have to be her and not Mr. Denton? she thought.

And then she had to smile to herself. If this worked, who better to see it all than Ms. Quelling, who thought the Corn Pops were perfect?

A rustling sound behind her interrupted Sophie's thoughts. Sophie rose up to see, and then she flattened herself again. The Corn Pops were arriving from the other direction.

"Are you ready, Antoinette?" she whispered to herself.

Her heart pounding, Sophie got up and began to deliver her lines down into the trench in a stage-loud voice.

"Don't fret, Private! I've bandaged your wound! It should hold until this final battle is over!"

It was pretty convincing, Sophie knew. She definitely wanted to make the Corn Pops think she wasn't aware they were there. But she couldn't hear them over her own voice. That was one thing she hadn't thought of. She knew Fiona would have.

Sophie shook her head under her mobcap and went into pantomime. Beyond her, Kitty's voice was fragile, but loud—and upset—enough to hear.

"Just leave me alone!" she cried.

"We just want to talk to you," B.J. said. "Come here!"

"We're going to give you one more chance." It was Anne-Stuart this time.

"No!" Kitty said. "You'll just play a trick on me!"

Their voices were getting closer. Sophie's heart pounded harder, but she just pantomimed in bigger gestures. It wasn't time to make her move yet.

Julia's voice rose over Kitty's, silky and smooth. "We don't play tricks. Sometimes we joke around—private jokes. You're just too sensitive."

"I just don't know when you're joking. It seems mean to me."

Uh-oh, Sophie thought. It sounded like Kitty might be giving in.

"We're not joking right now," Julia said. Her voice was like pancake syrup.

"In fact," Anne-Stuart said, "we're all going to swear a friendship oath and we want you to do it too."

By now it was obvious that they had stopped moving. *Don't listen to them, Kitty!* Sophie wanted to call to her. She bit down on her lip and pretended to watch anxiously for Lafayette over the horizon. She was careful not to look straight at the group.

"Why do you need an oath?" Kitty said.

"Well," Julia said. "Some people have been telling our group's secrets."

Sophie recognized Anne-Stuart's sniffle. "You know, like about our private jokes."

"We don't know who it is," Julia went on, "so we're *all* going to swear an oath."

"We're not going to cut ourselves or anything," B.J. said.

"Gro-oss!" Sophie was sure that was Willoughby.

"Then *what*, Julia?" Kitty said.

"We are all going to cut our hair *really* short."

"No, you're not!"

"Yes, we are," said Anne-Stuart. "We'll all help each other do it."

"I don't think I want to do that. I look awful with short hair!"

"Kitty!" Julia's voice almost sounded genuinely hurt. "Do you think I would make you look ugly? We're all still going to be cute."

"You'll be adorable," Anne-Stuart said. "And everybody else will start wearing theirs the same way."

Sophie heard the *snap snapping* of something metal.

"I've got the scissors," B.J. said. "They're exactly the kind stylists use."

"If you don't trust me, Kitty—" Julia sounded as if she were purring, "I guess I'll understand. You can do your own then. I'll hold your ponytail for you, and you can just—"

"No!"

Sophie went down on one knee. Kitty was coming closer again, and fast, and Sophie didn't want to mess things up now.

"If you can't take the oath with the rest of us," Julia said, "then maybe you're the one who told our secrets to somebody."

Her voice was coming closer too, but Sophie kept on acting and didn't look.

"Nooo!" Kitty said, closer still.

"Then what's the problem?" Anne-Stuart said. She was obviously right on Kitty's heels.

"Here, you want the scissors?" B.J. said.

There was an awful pause.

"Give them to me then," Julia said.

"Nooo!"

That's it, Sophie thought.

And then it was no longer just a plan. It was real, and it was happening.

Sophie sprang up, sweeping her bedspread cloak out to her sides, and shrieked "Kitty! Over here!"

Kitty ran the few steps it took to get to her, and Sophie folded her into the cloak and pushed the whole bundle behind her.

The Corn Pops were running too fast to stop. All four of them stumbled over the redoubt. Julia sprawled headlong, scissors flying from her hand.

Sophie scooped them up and held them over her head.

"Forfeit your recognizance, Redcoats!" she shouted. "We have got you handsomely in a pudding bag!"

B.J. still managed to say, "What?"

"You've been evil to Kitty for the last time," Sophie told them. She could feel Kitty shivering against her back, still cocooned inside the bedspread. "I *know* your secret. Your power is lost. The war is *over*!"

"What's going on over here?"

Sophie had never been so glad to see a teacher, even if it was Ms. Quelling.

"She's trying to attack us with scissors!" Julia cried. She pointed up at Sophie, who was still holding them up out of reach.

"Don't even try it, Julia," Sophie said. Her voice sounded like somebody else's, coming out of her own mouth. "She saw you go after Kitty with them."

"I didn't see anything except these girls all huddled together like they always are," Ms. Quelling said.

"You didn't see them threatening to cut off all of Kitty's hair?" Sophie said.

"No—where *is* Kitty?"

Sophie slowly stepped aside, her heart diving for the pit of her stomach. Kitty clung to her like a baby koala.

"I was trying to protect her," Sophie said.

"From whom?"

"From them!" Sophie pointed with the scissors at the Corn Pops.

"Let me have those before somebody puts an eye out," Ms. Quelling said.

Sophie handed them over and then put both arms around Kitty so she herself wouldn't shake.

"Thank you, Ms. Quelling," Anne-Stuart said breathlessly. She reached down to help Julia up and deposited her into B.J.'s waiting arms. "We were so scared."

"We were just playing around," Julia said, "and all of a sudden, Sophia was all grabbing at Kitty and waving those scissors around, saying she was going to cut *our* hair off."

Ms. Quelling looked at Sophie. "Is that true?" she said.

The only thing that kept Sophie from retreating back to Antoinette-land was the fact that Ms. Quelling actually looked surprised.

"No, it isn't true," Sophie said.

"Yes, it is," Julia said.

Kitty whimpered.

"Don't worry," Sophie said to her.

"You promised me," Kitty said. And then she really started to cry.

"You know we wouldn't hurt anybody, Ms. Quelling," Julia said. "You've known us since we were in kindergarten." She looked at Sophie and then at Kitty. "I don't mean to be rude, but both of them just moved here in the last six months. We don't know anything about *them*."

"Don't start talking like a York County aristocrat," Ms. Quelling said. "I don't think I can stomach it. At any rate, that doesn't prove a thing." She looked at everybody. "I can smell the fear in Kitty. She's so frightened of somebody that she's probably terrified to tell me which of you it is."

Sophie stole a glance at the Corn Pops. They were all open-mouthed, as if they couldn't believe Ms. Quelling wasn't hauling Sophie off to the office that very second.

"You know what really gets me?" Ms. Quelling said instead. "What really gets me is that any one of you would resort to behave this way toward people who are supposed to be your friends. You are intimidating AND manipulating. Teachers are always complaining about the boys who bully—but at least we can *see* what they're doing. Your business is secretive, and it's nasty—and it's deplorable. Do you know what that means, girls?"

Sophie was pretty sure she knew. It was heinous.

"I wish I did have proof," Ms. Quelling said, "because I suppose that's the only way we can put a stop to this—by making an example of someone."

"I have proof," said a voice.

It was a voice Sophie would have known even if she hadn't seen the wonderful gray eyes and the hair hanging over one eye. Fiona dropped neatly over the fence and walked past Sophie and Kitty, straight to Ms. Quelling. She was holding something behind her back.

"You were hiding and spying on us?" B.J. said. "That's not fair!"

"Yes, I was spying," Fiona said. "And how is that any more not fair than you trying to get Kitty to cut her hair just so you could humiliate her *again*?" Fiona looked at Ms. Quelling. "That's what happened. I saw the whole thing."

"You can't believe her," Anne-Stuart said. She was whining worse than Willoughby. "She's Sophie's best friend."

"Yeah, and you can't trust her," B.J. said. "She hung out with us all day all pretending to want to be our friend—and now we find out it was just so she could listen to our plans."

"Shut *up*!" Julia and Anne-Stuart shouted at her.

Ms. Quelling put both hands up and turned to Fiona. "Can you assure me that you are telling the truth?"

"I can do better than that," Fiona said. "I can prove it to you." From behind her back, she pulled what Sophie now saw was a video camera.

"I've got it all right here," Fiona said. "Want to watch it?"

It really was over after that. By the time they had all watched the mini-screen in the principal's office, the Corn Pops were all bawling their eyes out. Principal Olinghouse dismissed Kitty, Sophie, and Fiona.

Out in the hallway, Kitty stood alone like a red-eyed baby bird.

"So—do I get to be a Corn Flake?" she said. "I don't care if it does mean I have to be weird."

Sophie gave her an Antoinette smile. "You can be anything you want when you're a Corn Flake. That's the beauty of it."

"Do I have to swear an oath or anything?"

"No," Sophie said. "You just have to let your imagination run free. You can imagine anything."

Kitty gave a nervous-sounding giggle. "I guess I could try. I've gotta go, okay?" She skittered down the hall and disappeared through the double doors.

"What about me?"

Sophie turned to look at Fiona. For the first time, she realized Fiona had tears smeared on her face.

"What about me?" Fiona said again. "Can I be a Corn Flake again?"

Sophie swallowed hard. "Do you want to be?" she said.

"I do—but only if you want me." Fiona shoved aside the strand of hair that was sticking to her wet cheek. "I knew I did wrong, like the minute I hung up on you. Boppa came into my room and found me crying, and I told him what happened, and *he* told me I should apologize to you and make it right, only—I was just afraid you wouldn't take me back. So I hung out with the Corn Pops to find out what was going to happen—so I could prove to you—"

"That you're still my best friend?" Sophie said.

Fiona's face crumpled. All she could do was nod.

"And I'm yours," Sophie said. "That's all I care about, Henriette."

"Me too, Antoinette."

Then they hugged and did the secret handshake. And then they promised to share it with Kitty the first chance they got, since she obviously needed the Corn Flakes as much as they did.

By the time Fiona left school in the SUV and Sophie went to call Mama, she was very tired—maybe too tired for everything that was still ahead of her, even after this victory.

There would be Daddy's reaction to Dr. Peter's talk with him. That probably wasn't going to be fun. And then explaining all of this to Mama and Daddy—and maybe hearing Daddy say Sophie had gone too far.

Plus trying to adjust to having Kitty and her spacey-ness around. *And* figuring out how to stop Maggie from hating them.

Antoinette reached out her hand and smiled from within the folds of her black velvet hood. "Why don't you go to Jesus?" she said. "He'll show you—"

And so, of course, Sophie did. And there was no need for anyone to cough him away.

Glossary

amie {AH-mee} French word that means "female friend"

contempt {kuhn-TEMPT} the act of being hateful

countenance {KOWN-tuhn-nuhnce} old-fashioned word that means face or facial expression; usually means your mood can be seen on your face

deplorable {dih-PLORE-uh-buhl} so bad that has to be fixed or changed

feasible {FEE-zuh-buhl} can be done; is doable

heinous {HAY-nuhss} unbelievably mean and cruel, or beyond rude

hors d'oeuvres {or-DURVS} French words that aren't pronounced the French way, but it means fancy little snacks

immense {IH-mentz} great or big, or enormously huge

imperious {ihm-PEER-ee-uhss} snooty, like someone who thinks he or she is better than everybody else

intimidating {ihn-TIH-muh-date-ing} making somebody scared with threats or making someone feel like he or she isn't as good as you are

intrigued {ihn-TREEGD} very interested in something; really curious

ma {mah} French word that means "my"

manipulating {muh-NIP-you-late-ing} when someone is turning things around to get what he or she wants, often in a sneaky, unfair, or not truthful way

manipulator {muh-NIP-you-later} somebody who is manipulating

mundane {muhn-DAYN} ordinary, commonplace, bo-orrring

pantomime {PANT-uh-mime} the art of telling or acting out a story without speaking, using just body movements instead

pathetic {puh-THEH-tick} really pitiful, or kind of sad

pessimistic {PEH-suh-MISS-tick} really negative or letting gloomy thoughts take over good thoughts; always seeing the bad side

privy {PRIH-vee} when somebody knows a secret

recognizance {rih-CAHG-nuh-zuntz} promising to appear in court; the court says it trusts you will come back. If you forfeit it (disobey), you have to pay a bunch of money.

serviette {serve-YET} French word that means "napkin"

thoracic {thuh-RAA-sick} of, about, or inside the thorax, which is the part of your body between your neck and stomach; it's like your chest cavity where your heart and lungs are

Sophie's Secret

One

Y ou can't IMAGINE what it was like!" the tour guide said in a voice that echoed over the James River like a cranky old aunt.

Huh, thought Sophie. *Maybe YOU can't imagine it, Mister Mouth—but I can!*

Sophie LaCroix pulled her black wool cape around her—the one Mama had made for her just for this sightseeing trip—and tried to bunch her long, not-quite-blonde-not-quite-brown hair into the hood to muffle Mr. Mouth's voice. How was she supposed to concentrate on the delicious real-ness of Jamestown Island with this guy barging into the quiet, telling her that she, Sophie LaCroix, "couldn't imagine".

Imagining is my specialty, she wanted to inform him. *Have YOU ever imagined YOURself back in the eighteenth century, acted it out, and made a film of it?* Sophie sniffed. *Probably NOT.*

She edged away from the guide and gazed across the river. In the film they'd just watched in the Visitors' Center—well, SHE and Mama had actually watched it while her thirteen-year-old sister Lacie and Aunt Bailey had made fun of the nar-rator talking like he had a chip bag clip on his nose—the narrator's voice had described the river as "a salty brine at high tide and a blend of slime and filth at low." Sophie wanted to repeat this to her best friend, Fiona, back at school, and maybe they could start saying that about the Poquoson River in THEIR town. It would sound so cool. So would "the drear, dark sky"—which did stretch over the river on that day after Thanksgiving and slowly soak them with drizzle. Mama had wanted her to put on a plastic poncho, but that would totally ruin the effect of the cape.

Besides, Sophie thought, *I'm sure Captain John Smith didn't have a plastic raincoat back in 1607.* No, this experience had to be as real as she could make it—so she and Fiona and Kitty could develop their next movie around it.

Because, of course, that's what they—the Corn Flakes—would have to do as soon as Thanksgiving vacation was over. A "cheerless sky" and the possibility of cruel diseases "such as swellings, fluxes, and burning fevers" like the film had described: that stuff was too good to waste. Sophie stretched out her hands to the river.

Antoinette called silently to God to help her know the secrets that lay at the slimy, filthy river bottom. Antoinette's heart began to pound as she found herself at the brink of some new mission— some fascinating adventure—some brilliant endeavor that would make Papa see once and for all that she was worthy of his honor and respect—

"Soph—what are you doing?"

Sophie felt a heavy hand on her shoulder, and she had to scurry back from Antoinette's world to focus up at her father. He was towering over her, and nobody could tower like way-tall Daddy with his broad, I-used-to-be-a-football-star shoulders and his sharp blue eyes, so unlike Sophie's soft brown ones. In fact, Sophie always thought that if somebody lined up a dozen fathers and asked a stranger to pick out which one was hers, they'd never get the right one.

"We're all headed up to the fort," Daddy said.

"Can't I just stay and look at the river for a couple more minutes?" Sophie said.

Daddy shook his big dark head. "No, because next thing I know you'll be in it. We're working as a team today."

Sophie muttered an "okay" and tried to wriggle her shoulder out of his hand, but he had the Daddy Grip on it.

"No way, Soph," he said. "I don't want a repeat of that Williamsburg thing."

Sophie didn't remind him that she had grown WAY up since THAT happened back in September. *What would be the point?* she thought as she broke into a jog to keep up with him. *He thinks I'm the biggest ditz in the universe and he always will. And it's SO not fair!*

"I wish you would've let me bring my video camera," she said.

Daddy gave a grunt. "Uh-huh—then I'd have to keep you on a leash." He stopped about six feet from a statue where Mama, Sophie's little brother Zeke, Lacie, and Aunt Bailey and Uncle Preston were gathered.

Wonderful, Sophie thought. *He's going to give me a lecture right here where they can all hear.* She wished she'd never asked the question.

At least Daddy squatted down in front of her, so his voice wouldn't boom down to her tiny height, but he still didn't let go of her shoulder. It was all she could do not to squirm.

"Look, we've had this discussion before," he said.

Yeah, about sixty bajillion times, Sophie thought.

"Everything is not always all about you," he went on.

It NEVER is!

"We're here to do what Aunt Bailey and Uncle Preston want to do, because they're our guests. I don't think that includes

137

standing there watching you stare at the river for an hour, dreaming up trouble."

Sophie straightened her thin shoulders under Daddy's hand. "I was starting an idea for our next film."

"Well, take notes or something." Daddy stood up. "Are you going to stay with the team, or do I have to hold your hand like a little kid? That would be pretty embarrassing for an eleven-year-old."

That was actually a tough question. Sophie did NOT want to be on any kind of "team" with her own sister, much less her aunt and uncle. But the thought of trailing behind her father all day was worse. She gave a sigh that came from her heels and blew the little wisps of hair on her forehead. It wasn't wasted on Daddy.

"Don't be a drama queen about it," he said, eyes narrowed. "Just think of it as taking a hit for the team." He nodded toward the statue. "Let's go."

Sophie waited until he finally let go of her shoulder, and then she squared herself off again and headed toward the "team."

Antoinette tossed back her long, luxurious hair and put on a smile. She couldn't let Papa take away the chance to pay her respects to her ancestor, Captain John Smith. He wasn't French like she was, of course, but she thought of him as her forefather because he, like her, had been a pioneer, a taker of risks, a person who stood up against things more evil than good —

"Oh wow — he was a total BABE!"

Sophie glared at Lacie.

"I mean, look at that BODY," Lacie said. She was gaping up at the statue.

Aunt Bailey sidled up next to Lacie. "That's what I'M talkin' about."

Five-year-old Zeke furrowed his little dark brows at Aunt Bailey. "WHAT are you talkin' about?" he said.

Mama cocked her head, all curly with frosted hair, and gave Sophie's aunt a hard look. "Thank you, Bailey," she said.

Aunt Bailey covered her very red lips with her hand — with nails all squared off and white at the tips — and giggled in Lacie's direction. Although Aunt Bailey was OLD, like probably thirty, Sophie thought she acted like she was Lacie's age.

"That's John Smith, Z," Daddy said to Zeke. "You remember him from Pocahontas?"

"Oh, yeah," Zeke said. He cocked his head just the way Mama did, though his hair was dark like Daddy's, and it stood straight up in coarse, little spikes on his head. "Did they get married?"

"Nah," Daddy said. "They might have gone out a few times, but she married somebody else."

"She married John Rolfe, Daddy," Sophie said. "And I'm SURE she never went on a date with Captain John Smith."

Uncle Preston gave Daddy a nudge with his elbow. "Silly you," he said to him.

Then Daddy gave one of those only-one-side-of-his-mouth-going-up smiles that made Sophie want to punch something. *He might as well just come right out and SAY I'm a little know-it-all*, Sophie thought. *Because that's what he thinks.*

"Watch your tone, Sophie," Daddy said.

WHAT tone? Sophie thought. *I was just sharing information!*

"All right, folks, now if you'll just follow me," Mr. Mouth was saying, "I'm going to take you to the 1607 James Fort site. I think you'll be fascinated by what I have to tell you." He puffed up his chest.

"Now, the question many folks ask me is, why do we need to dig up remnants of a civilization that no longer exists?"

"That would be MY question," Lacie muttered to Aunt Bailey. They rolled their eyes in unison.

"Here is the best answer I can give you," Mr. Mouth went on. "The present is better understood when viewed through the lenses of the past—"

Sophie jerked her head around, so that her face was sideways in the hood. Even before she could straighten it out, her mind was teeming.

The lenses of the past! she thought. *The lenses of my camera— that's what they are: "the lenses of the past."*

She really did wish she could take notes—although she was pretty sure she would remember a gem like THAT. Fiona was going to be so impressed.

Sophie stood on a low concrete wall so she could get a better view of Mr. Mouth. He was now shouting like Lacie's soccer coach, but at least he was finally saying something she wanted to hear.

"That's why it's so significant for archaeologists here at Jamestown to find, for instance, the remains of the fort," he said, "because it was the center of their life, and this is where they set the precedents for our representative government and legal code."

Sophie didn't know what "precedents" were, but she was sure Fiona would. She stood on her tiptoes to see where Mr. Mouth was now pointing. There were several men wearing hard hats and very dirty clothes, down on their hands and knees, making tiny digs in the dirt with pointed instruments that looked like pens.

"You can see how precise the techniques are," Mr. Mouth said. "But this is the way they discovered the rest of the palisade of the fort. It's called a trenching technique. They're following the white blocks in the ground where they think the palisades were."

"Whatever," Lacie mumbled. Aunt Bailey, of course, nodded. Sophie moved a few more inches away from them on top of the low wall and craned her neck to see the map Mr. Mouth was holding.

"We know where to dig for PHYSICAL evidence—such as building ruins and artifacts—by using the DOCUMENTARY evidence we find. This is a map left by one of the secretaries of the first General Assembly, giving the measurements!"

Mr. Mouth was so delighted with THAT piece of information, he sprayed the people who were standing directly in front of him with enthusiastic spit.

"Gross me out," Lacie whispered to Aunt Bailey.

"We might need those plastic ponchos after all," Aunt Bailey whispered back.

Mama turned and gave Lacie a don't-be-disrespectful look. Sophie would have taken a minute to enjoy that if she hadn't wanted to hear every word Mr. Mouth was saying. She decided to call him Mr. Messenger instead.

He's like a messenger of knowledge from the past, she thought. She KNEW Fiona would be impressed with THAT.

"These archaeologists have uncovered over three hundred and fifty thousand artifacts dating to the first half of the seventeenth century," Mr. Messenger said. "They have even excavated two large trash pits."

"They dug through the garbage?" Lacie said.

This time it didn't come out in a whisper, and Mr. Messenger turned to her with wide eyes, as if he were overjoyed that she'd asked that question.

"Yes, young lady!" he said. "You would be amazed what we can learn about a society from its refuse. In fact, well-preserved trash is a Jamestown treasure!"

Sophie made a mental note of that. Lacie turned to Aunt Bailey and wrinkled her nose.

"I don't think I'd want to know THAT bad," she murmured.

"As you can see," Mr. Messenger said, "they are still working. Where I'm going to take you next, they are excavating what may have been a graveyard."

"This just keeps getting better and better," Aunt Bailey whispered. "First old garbage, now dead bodies."

"And then we'll watch the further excavation of a well," Mr. Messenger continued. "They've already found a metal armor breastplate—"

"Now THAT's a bra," Aunt Bailey said behind her hand to Lacie. "Speaking of bras, we need to go shopping. I know you're wearing the wrong size right now."

Sophie could feel her face going crimson. She checked out her parents to see if they were hearing all this, but Mama was deep in conversation with one of the archaeologists, and Daddy was watching Mama, his arms folded and his head bent toward Uncle Preston.

"What do you want to bet Lynda is at this moment giving that guy directions to our home?" Sophie heard Daddy say, "The woman never meets a stranger."

Mr. Messenger was winding up his explanation before they moved on, and Sophie was now having a harder time focusing on him with all those other conversations going on around her. She leaned out just a tiny bit more.

"When we go into the tent where the archaeologists are working on the well site," Mr. Messenger said, "you will see them using very small trowels to scrape one eighth of an inch of earth at a time and then sweep it into five gallon buckets. All that dirt goes through a screen—"

"Uh-oh," Daddy said to Uncle Preston. "There go all my buckets. Lynda will be down here tomorrow with ten of them and a half a dozen gardening shovels."

Daddy! Sophie wanted to shout at him. *I can't concentrate!*

She leaned out just a little more—and suddenly she was on the ground, tumbling down the incline toward the river.

She tried to grab onto something to stop herself, but she was tangled up in her cape, and half the hood was covering her face. Arms flailing, she knew she had to be within inches of the water, and all she could think was, *If I fall in, I'm going to be in SO much trouble!*

And then something stopped her, and Sophie clung to it with both cape-entangled arms. With a jerk of her neck, she got the hood off her face and found herself looking up at Mr. Messenger. She was hanging onto his legs.

It was the closest she had been to him, and now she could see that his eyes were twinkling.

"No swimming allowed, missy," he said.

He gave her a grin and a hand to haul herself up with. She dusted off her cape, and then she curtsied.

"Thank you, kind sir," she said.

He dipped into a deep bow. "You are quite welcome, m'lady."

Behind her, Sophie could hear Lacie wailing, "She did NOT just curtsy to that guy!"

And she could hear Zeke yelling, "Mama! Sophie almost fell in the water!"

But all she really LISTENED to were the words of Mr. Messenger as he smiled down at her.

"You are a student of history, aren't you?" he said.

"I am. I make my own historical films—well, with my friends."

"And I imagine they are spectacular. How would you like to take a peek under these tarps here and see the chimney foundation and the floorboards of a house they've found?"

Sophie looked over at an area as big as their garage at home that was covered with a sheet of thick green plastic, and her heart started to pound.

"Oh, yes, sir, please!" Antoinette cried. She clasped the kind man's hands in hers and looked up with tears shining in her eyes. "I would give anything to know more about those brave men and women who came before me and suffered so much for this new land—"

"You better keep an eye on her, Rusty—she'll go off with anybody!"

Sophie turned to glare at Uncle Preston, but there wasn't even time to narrow her eyes. Daddy suddenly had her by the arm, pulling her hands away from Mr. Messenger.

"That's okay," Daddy said to him. "We're headed off for the gift shop. We have a lot of ground to cover today."

With that, he dragged Sophie away. She barely got a wave in to Mr. Messenger before Daddy was halfway into a lecture. Something about never being able to take her anywhere because she wasn't a team player.

Sophie didn't hear most of it. She let her eyes, and her ears, glaze over.

TWO

All the way back to Poquoson, while Lacie and Aunt Bailey talked about how they wouldn't have wanted to live in the seventeenth century because there were no malls, and Uncle Preston flipped through radio stations trying to get the Texas game, Sophie stared out at the drizzle and did what she did best. She imagined. *I can't be Antoinette AND be an archaeologist*, she thought. *But I can be LIKE Antoinette and Captain John Smith: I will be a pioneer for all that has more good than evil.*

Then she dreamed some more until she came up with the perfect name: Dr. Demetria Diggerty.

Of course, Sophie knew she would have to give Dr. Diggerty more than just a name, and to do that she needed quiet time in her room. So it really didn't bother her that almost as soon as they got back to the house late that afternoon, she heard Aunt Bailey and Lacie go off to the movies without inviting her. What DID bother her was that the minute the house was quiet, with Mama and Zeke off to the grocery store to buy stuff for supper and Uncle Preston dozing in front of a football game on TV, Daddy came immediately to Sophie's room.

Sophie curled WAY up on the purple rug in the library corner of her room. Daddy didn't waste any words. He didn't even sit down.

"Look," he said, pointing at her from his towering height, "I'm trying to understand you, Sophie. I've had the sessions with Dr. Peter, I got you the camera, and I'll let you keep it as long as you keep improving in school."

He paused, and since Sophie didn't know what she was supposed to say, she just shrugged.

"What does that mean?" Daddy said.

"It means I don't know what to say."

"You don't know what to say when I give you all that lee-way and you still abuse it?"

Now Sophie REALLY didn't know what to say. She didn't even understand what he was talking about.

"I asked you to *stay* with the group and I *told* you why." Daddy was poking his finger toward her, one jab for each word that came out louder than the rest. "But could you *do* that? *No.* The *first* chance you got, you were *hanging* back with the guide, acting like one of your *pretend* characters. We don't *know* that man, *Sophie.* You don't go *grabbing* onto STRANGERS!"

Sophie plastered herself against the wall. She hadn't seen Daddy this mad since the day Zeke had "run away from home" to hide underneath the workbench in the garage. Sophie had found him and gotten him to pretend with her that they were like wounded soldiers coming home after a war so she could get him out. Only they got so wrapped up in the game, Sophie forgot to tell anybody where they were, and Mama was just calling the police when Lacie located them. Just like then, Daddy's face was now scarlet, and his eyes were in sharp points of blue. Sophie swallowed hard.

"Do you understand why I'm so upset with you?" Daddy said.

Sophie didn't, but she nodded anyway. He paused for a long time, and when she couldn't stand it any more, she said, "What's my punishment going to be?"

"You're already having it," he said. "I wouldn't let Bailey take you to the movies with Lacie."

It was all Sophie could do not to break into the biggest grin ever. She bit at her lip and gave him a solemn nod.

"I want you to sit in here tonight and think about what happens when you're not aware of your surroundings." Her father's voice was still stern, but at least he'd stopped poking his finger at her. "The whole purpose of giving you that camera was so you would limit your daydreaming to filming."

Sophie opened her mouth to say, "If you would've just let me TAKE the camera WITH me"—but she decided against it. Daddy's face was returning to its natural color. It was better not to take any chances.

"Think about it," he said to her. "And for the rest of the weekend, I'd better see some improvement in your being a team player, or I WILL take that camera away."

When Daddy closed the door behind him on his way out, Sophie was sure that HER face was scarlet.

Dr. Demetria Diggerty wouldn't put up with treatment like that, she wanted to scream. *SHE knows more about palisades and trenching techniques and metal armor breastplates than ANYBODY, including HIM. Nobody makes her feel like SHE's a moron—because she isn't.*

Dr. Peter—that was Sophie's therapist, and the coolest one she was sure, even though she didn't know any other psychologists—had taught her that when she got mad at her father or anybody else that she should imagine Jesus, not Antoinette, and she was pretty sure that applied to Dr. Demetria Diggerty too. The Jesus in her mind, with his kind eyes, could always make her calm down and not hurl books across the room, and eventually she would know what to do.

But right now, she really didn't want Jesus to see her with her fists clenched and her head about to explode. It seemed safer to imagine what Dr. Diggerty looked like ...

She would have to have short hair, swept back so it didn't get in her way when she was digging up Jamestown treasure, but still romantic—maybe with some streaks in it or something. And her eyes—they would be brown and intelligent and able to see what she was going to find even before she found it. She was that in tune with the earth and all that it was hiding about the past.

The next morning Sophie wanted to call Fiona as soon as she got up so they could start planning their film—a documentary on excavating Jamestown. Then she remembered that Fiona and her family were at Club Med for the weekend, and Kitty and the rest of the Munfords were away visiting grandparents. Sophie would have settled for curling up by the fireplace in the family room all day and reading the book Mama had bought at the Jamestown gift shop to get more ideas—but at breakfast, Aunt Bailey announced that she was taking the "women" shopping. One glance at Daddy, and Sophie knew she'd better not protest.

While he and Uncle Preston and Zeke took off to shoot baskets at the gym, Sophie piled into their old Suburban with the other "women." Mama looked about as excited about it as Sophie did, and she barely spoke a syllable the whole way there.

Who can get a word in anyway? Sophie thought. *Aunt Bailey and Lacie never shut up!*

And they didn't the whole time they were shopping. It was the WORST when they went to the lingerie department at Dillard's. Sophie remembered too late that Aunt Bailey had told Lacie they were going to buy her new bras, or Sophie would have faked diarrhea and begged Mom to take her to the ladies' room. By the time she realized what was happening, Aunt Bailey had already borrowed a tape measure from the sales clerk and was wrapping it around Lacie's chest.

"You have such a cute figure, Lacie," Aunt Bailey said as she gave the tape a professional snap. "I don't think the bras you're wearing are showing it off at all."

"I think the bras she's wearing are just fine," Mama said. Her elfin lips were tight. They reminded Sophie of the top of a drawstring bag.

"A good bra is definitely expensive," Aunt Bailey said. "But don't worry about the price, Lynda. I'm treating."

Lacie held her arms out for Aunt Bailey to reposition the tape measure under her breasts. Sophie wanted to go through the floor, but it didn't seem to be bothering Lacie at all.

"Aunt Bailey can afford it, Mama," Lacie said. "She and Uncle Preston are DINKS."

"What?" Mama said.

"Double Income, No Kids," Lacie said.

"That's right," Aunt Bailey said. "So let me treat the girl to a nice foundation garment or two." She suddenly swept her eyes, bright blue in her colored contacts, over Sophie. "I would buy Sophie some too, but I don't see any signs of development there at all."

Sophie crossed her arms over her chest and felt her face going BEYOND scarlet.

"She's a late bloomer," Mama said. She put her arm around Sophie's shoulders.

"Still," Aunt Bailey said. She tilted her head, its hair gelled into a dozen auburn flips, and gave Sophie a thorough going-over with her eyes. "She could use a little padded bra. That would be cute."

"No!" Sophie said. "I'm not gonna pretend I have breasts when I don't!"

"Why not?" Lacie said. "You pretend everything else."

"Lacie, that's enough," Mama said. "You two do the bra thing. Sophie and I are going to look around."

"Mama babies her so much," Sophie heard Lacie say to Aunt Bailey as she and Mama moved away. Sophie didn't look back at them, but she was sure Aunt Bailey was nodding and rolling her eyes.

"I'm not a baby," Sophie said to Mama when they were safely in the pajama aisle. "I just don't need a bra."

"No, you don't," Mama said. The drawstring mouth was loosening up, but only a little.

"I don't even see what good breasts do until you have babies and stuff anyway."

Mama even smiled then, in that impish way she had that Sophie loved. "I'm happy to hear that. But I don't want you to feel left out, since Lacie is getting something."

"I'd rather have a trowel," Sophie said.

Mama's eyebrows went up as if she'd just made a discovery. "Ah, so that's what you're dreaming up now. You and the girls going to make the next Indiana Jones movie?"

Sophie shook her head firmly. "Better than Indiana Jones. We're going to be girl archaeologists and make amazing discoveries. That's why I need a trowel."

But they didn't have trowels in Dillard's, and since they were only going into stores Aunt Bailey wanted to go into, Mama suggested a couple of pretty little camisoles for Sophie to wear under her clothes, now that the weather was getting colder and she needed layers. "Since you don't have any body fat," Mama said.

Sophie tried on the camisoles, and she did have to admit they felt silky and good next to her skin, sort of grown-up. She was pretty sure Dr. Demetria Diggerty would wear something like that.

Later, when they were waiting for Aunt Bailey to decide between four different pairs of black boots, with Lacie's help, Mama put her arm around Sophie again and whispered to her that every girl developed at a different rate. That helped when, after purchasing three of the four pairs of boots, Aunt Bailey treated them to TCBY and went on about how gorgeous Lacie was becoming until Sophie was too nauseous to even eat her chocolate and vanilla swirl with gummy bears.

When Sunday came, Sophie stood on the front porch and made sure Daddy was REALLY going to take Aunt Bailey and Uncle Preston to the airport. Sophie had never been so happy to see somebody leave.

Monday morning on the bus, Sophie had no sooner pulled out her planning notebook to dream up some more details about Dr. Diggerty when the two girls in front of her turned around, up on their knees, to face her.

"Hey," one of them said.

Sophie knew both their names because they were in her class, although they had never really talked to her much until she had started riding the bus a few weeks before. The one in the Redskins sweatshirt was Harley Hunter. Her friend was Gillian Cooper, only everybody called her "Gill" with a hard "G" like in "girl."

Harley was sort of husky and she was always grinning, so that her cheeks came up and made her eyes almost disappear. Her sandy hair was cut short, and she gelled it so it would stand up.

It was hard to remember that Gill even HAD hair, because she wore a hat as often as she could get away with it. Today her reddish hair, which was as lanky as her long body, was tucked up into a green newsboy cap, the kind Daddy always said looked like an old-fashioned golfer's hat. It matched her green fleece jacket and her eyes.

"Hey," Sophie said back to them. And then she couldn't think what else to say. Gill and Harley were two of the four jock girls in her class, all into sports, and Sophie was always afraid they'd be like Lacie and start bugging her because she didn't play soccer or something.

"Me and her have been talking," Gill said, jabbing a thumb in Harley's direction, "and we decided you rock."

For a few seconds, Sophie could only stare. She finally found enough of her high-pitched little voice to say, "I rock? How come?"

"You and Fiona took DOWN the popular girls," Gill said. "You didn't let them run over you like they do everybody else."

Sophie knew they were talking about the Corn Pops, as she and Fiona and Kitty—the Corn *Flakes*—referred to them in private. They were the pretty, smart, everybody-likes-me girls led by queen bee Julia Cummings. She had three worker bees—B.J. Freeman, Anne-Stuart Riggins, and Willoughby Wiley. There had been a fourth one until Kitty had become a Corn Flake. She had almost had to, to protect herself against the Corn Pops. They weren't the sweetest box of cereal on the shelf.

Gill gave Sophie a friendly punch on the arm. "You even made the teachers see that those girls aren't all that, the way they always thought they were since, like, kindergarten."

Harley punched Sophie's other shoulder. "You rock," she said.

I like rocking, Sophie decided as she got off the bus. *I think Dr. Demetria Diggerty rocks too, and people know it.*

Thinking of the good doctor, Sophie headed for the playground where Fiona and Kitty always waited for her before school, almost bursting open with what she knew Fiona would call "a scathingly brilliant idea." Fiona had the best vocabulary of any kid in sixth grade—or maybe even all of Great Marsh Elementary.

They were on the swings when she got there, and Sophie barely let them say hello before she was launching into details.

Fiona watched her carefully out of her wonderful gray eyes, one stream of golden-brown hair erupting from her knitted striped beanie cap and over the side of her face. Sophie always thought that piece of hair made her best friend look exotic.

Kitty followed Sophie with her eyebrows knit together over her big blue eyes like she wasn't quite getting it. When Sophie was finishing up the details, Kitty played nervously with her ponytail of ringlets.

"Are we going to have to act all weird when we make this movie?" she said. "It sounds like it."

Fiona pulled her lips into their perfect heart shape. "It isn't being weird," she said. "It's being an actor."

"I don't know if I can do that, though." Kitty's voice curled up into a whine. "I'll get all nervous."

"When you're yourself," Sophie said, "it's never weird. Remember—that's our Corn Flakes motto."

Kitty pressed her lips together until her dimples punctured her cheeks. Kitty, Sophie knew, still wasn't sure about being a full-fledged Corn Flake.

The bell rang and they hurried into the building, Sophie and Fiona already puzzling over exactly what was going to happen in their movie.

"I think we should do an actual dig," Fiona said. "And we can make the movie about the stuff we find."

"I LOVE that!" Sophie said.

"She LOVES that," someone said behind her, in a high-pitched voice that mocked Sophie's.

"If she loves it," someone else said, "then it's got to be something WAY lame."

Sophie didn't even have to turn around to know it was the Corn Pops.

Three

"I guess there aren't any teachers around," Fiona said to Sophie, so the Corn Pops couldn't miss it, "or they wouldn't be talking like that."

Sophie glanced down the hall. She could see the BACK of Mr. Denton's balding head gleaming in the overhead lights as he stood outside the door of the Language Arts room. That would explain why Julia was taking a chance being rude.

Still, Sophie thought, *Julia should be careful. If ANY of the Corn Pops are caught being evil, they're toast.*

Beside her, Kitty whimpered and clung to Sophie's arm. Fiona rolled her eyes.

"Kitty, when are you going to figure out that they can't hurt you anymore?" she said.

Fiona looked straight at Julia, who tossed her thick, auburn hair and let it bounce back into place across the shoulders of her red polo dress. It matched the one B.J. was wearing, only hers was dark blue. B.J. tossing HER shiny short bob of butter-blonde didn't have quite the same effect as when Julia did it, but, then, SHE wasn't the Queen Bee.

"Don't be so sure about that," B.J. said.

But the third Pop, Anne-Stuart, nudged her with a bony elbow and said, "When did we ever hurt Kitty to begin with?"

Sophie took another quick look back at Mr. Denton. He was turning their way, and all three of the Corn Pops' faces spread into practiced smiles.

"Whatever," Julia said, and she swept off down the hall with Anne-Stuart and B.J. behind her, still beaming at Mr. Denton.

"Are you three behaving yourselves?" he said as they hurried past him into the room.

"Yes, sir!" Anne-Stuart said. And then she gave a juicy sniff. Sophie always thought Anne-Stuart must have the worst sinuses in York County.

Fiona led the Corn Flakes toward the room, and they all grinned at Mr. Denton.

"Everything okay?" he said.

"YES," Sophie said, and she squeezed Kitty's hand.

Mr. Denton nodded. "You let me know if it isn't."

"See?" Fiona said to Kitty as they walked in. "You have absolutely nothing to worry about."

That was true, and Sophie knew it. HER only real worry was that she needed to improve by at least a point in each of her classes this week so she could keep on using her video camera. She was dying to try some of the old spellings of things she'd read about in her Jamestown book, like "meddows" and "blud" and "peece"—and her personal favorite, "dyinge," for "dying." But she decided this wasn't the time to have Mr. Denton counting off on her paper. She did manage to slip one of the new words she'd learned from the book—"vexations"—into one of her vocabulary word sentences, just to impress him.

At lunchtime that day, when Fiona, Kitty, and Sophie were settling in at their usual cafeteria table, Harley and Gill came up, zippered lunch bags in hand.

"Can we sit with you guys?" Gill said. She had taken off the green newsboy cap, and her hair was shoved back on one side with a barrette shaped like a soccer ball.

"Absolutely you can," Sophie said.

"Them too?" Harley said.

She jerked her spiky head back at their two friends that Sophie knew were named Nikki and Yvette, although she didn't know which was which because they were identical twins, with short blonder-than-blonde hair that they were always tucking behind their ears to keep it from falling into their faces.

"Y'all know Nikki and Yvette?" Sophie said to Kitty and Fiona.

"It's Vette," Gill informed them. "Like short for CORvette. They're very into cars."

"Can they talk?" Fiona said.

"Of course they can talk," Gill said.

"Just asking," Fiona said.

A conversation began about just how many cars the twins' dad had in his collection, but Sophie's attention wandered to the far end of the table, where a stocky girl with very dark chin-length hair and skin the color of pancake syrup was watching the Corn Flakes and the "jocks."

Maybe they could be the Wheaties, Sophie thought.

Then she grinned at the dark girl. "Hey, Maggie," she said. "Why don't you come down here and sit with us?"

"Because I don't want to be a Corn Flake," Maggie said.

As usual, every one of Maggie's words fell into the air like a bag of flour being dropped to the floor. Sophie sagged. That was the answer she always got, ever since she and Fiona had dumped Maggie a while back. Even though Sophie asked her to hang out with them about three times a week, Maggie always said the same thing. Mama had told Sophie that some people would hold a grudge forever.

Sophie felt a nudge in the back and turned to find a plastic container practically in her face.

"Want one?" Harley said.

"Her mom always starts baking Christmas cookies the day after Thanksgiving," Gill said. "Take one of the snowflakes. They, like, disappear in your mouth."

"I like these surprise bar things better," Fiona said. She was currently splitting one open to share with Kitty, who already had several dabs of chocolate on her upper lip.

"Harley doesn't share these with just anybody," Gill said. "This is 'cause you guys rock."

The belonging-feeling that Sophie suddenly had inside her chest was almost enough to make her want to go out for basketball or something, just for the Wheaties girls. She looked around the table at the six of them who surrounded her.

Who woulda thought just two months ago that I would have even ONE friend, much less this many? Sophie thought.

And even though they were all way different, everybody was getting along, which was the best part.

I betcha Dr. Peter would say this was like Jesus, she thought. *Sitting down at the table with all different people that nobody else understood.*

She would be seeing Dr. Peter the next day. She decided she'd have to tell him about this.

"Excuse me," somebody said in a sniffling voice.

"What do you want, Anne-Stuart?" Fiona said. She was never one for being friendlier to a Corn Pop than she had to be, even if the Pop was smiling like a packet of Sweet-and-Low the way Anne-Stuart was doing right now.

Anne-Stuart pulled her skinny self up to her tallest and gave her neck a nervous-looking jerk. It sent a ripple through the perfect sandy hair pulled back by a black suede headband, an exact match for her mini-skirt and boots. Sophie knew Aunt Bailey would have said that was NOT a good look for someone with legs that scrawny.

"I'm taking a survey," Anne-Stuart said. She tapped a pad of lavender lined paper with a perfectly sharpened pencil that didn't even have any teeth marks in it yet.

"What kind of survey?" Fiona said.

By now Kitty had her head buried behind Fiona's shoulder. Harley was straightening hers.

"I'm asking all the girls: who wears a bra and what size is it?"

"None of your business," Maggie said from the far end.

She shoved an uneaten banana into her lunch bag and got up and left.

Anne-Stuart appeared to be making a note on her pad, and then she looked expectantly at Gill.

"We all wear 'em," Gill said, pointing to the three Wheaties.

Anne-Stuart nodded and scribbled like she was taking down votes for the presidential election. "What sizes?" she said.

"Medium," Gill said, jabbing a finger toward Harley. "The rest of us wear smalls."

There was a thick sniff from Anne-Stuart. "Then you all don't really wear bras, or you would know that they don't come in small, medium, and large." She turned the pencil over impatiently and started to erase.

"Shows what you know," Gill said. "These are sports bras."

"Oh," Anne-Stuart said. She puckered her almost-invisible eyebrows in a frown and then looked at Fiona.

"I'm only telling you this because I know if you try to use it for something evil, you'll get kicked out of school," Fiona said. "I wear a thirty, double-A."

Sophie stared at her. She'd had no idea Fiona wore a bra. She suddenly felt like her own chest was shrinking.

"And you?" Anne-Stuart said, bulging her watery eyes at Kitty.

"Tell her, Kit," Fiona said, giving her a jab in the ribs Sophie could almost feel.

Kitty kept her gaze glued to the tabletop. "I wear a thirty-two, A," she said. Sophie could hardly hear her.

Anne-Stuart obviously did, because she pulled the pad into her chest and shook her head at Kitty. "You know that's not true," she said. "You can't possibly wear a bigger size bra than I do."

"What do you want her to do, pull off her sweater and show you the tag?" Fiona said.

"No!" Kitty said.

"No, I do not," Anne-Stuart said. "But I'm putting a question mark next to it."

Anne-Stuart made that notation with a flourish, and then she looked at Sophie. Her eyes were expectant, as if she had been saving the best for last.

"How about you, Sophie?" she said.

If I don't answer, Sophie thought, *Anne-Stuart will go back to the Corn Pops and tell them she had me scared or something. NO WAY!*

Still, she could feel her face burning as she adjusted her glasses on her nose and looked over the top of them at Anne-Stuart. "I prefer not to wear a bra," she said. "I wear a camisole."

Anne-Stuart gave the biggest snot-snort yet. "Doesn't have any breasts yet," she said as she wrote on her pad. Then she gave them her NutraSweet smile, turned on the heel of her black suede boot, and pranced to the Corn Pops table, where Julia, B.J., and Willoughby were sitting on the edges of their seats as if Anne-Stuart were going to come back and announce the Academy Award winners.

"They are just as heinous as they ever were," Fiona said. "I think we conducted ourselves like mature women."

Harley gave her a blank look. "Because I didn't get up and punch her out?" she said.

"Pretty much," Fiona said.

Sophie slid down in her seat and pulled open her turkey sandwich. Mama had put cranberry sauce on it, just the way she liked it, but she couldn't have eaten if she'd been starving to death.

Why did I get all embarrassed over that? she thought. *Stuff like body things never made me turn red before —*

At least until everybody on the planet started talking about the breasts I don't have!

"Hey, Soph."

Sophie looked up quickly at Fiona.

"We're over them," she said. She darted her eyes quickly at Kitty, who was cowering at Fiona's side.

"We are SO over them," Sophie said. She stretched so she could get closer to Kitty. "As a matter of fact, what was she talking about? I forget already."

"I'm thinking we should be concentrating on starting our movie after school," Fiona said.

Sophie gave her head a firm nod, the way she knew Dr. Demetria Diggerty would.

"The digging begins this afternoon—my backyard. Bring your trowels."

Four

*I*t *certainly couldn't be a more perfect day for a dig,* thought
Dr. Demetria Diggerty as she gathered the white buckets
and the trowels and headed for the site where her two eager
assistants were waiting to begin.

"What are your names?" Dr. Diggerty said.

"Artifacta Allen," said the mysterious one with the wonderful gray eyes.

"Kitty Munford," said the other one.

"No," Sophie said. She tried to keep her voice patient.
"What is your name going to be in the film?"

Kitty looked around blankly. "I don't see the camera."

"We have to plan first," Fiona said—LESS than patiently.

Sophie handed each of them one of Mama's small gardening shovels. She hadn't asked Mama if she could use them
before she left with Zeke to set up for the bake sale Lacie's
basketball team was having, but Sophie was sure it would be
okay. After all, Mama had been excited about Jamestown treasure herself.

"Just be thinking of a name, Kitty," Sophie said. "For now,
we'll just call you—"

"Kitty," Kitty said.

Sophie knelt down on the damp ground at the edge of the square she had drawn out in the dirt with a pointed stick in the back corner of the LaCroix's yard.

"According to the documental evidence I have obtained," Sophie—Dr. Demetria Diggerty—said, "this is a likely place to find artifacts."

"What's documental evidence?" Kitty said.

"You would already know that if you were an archaeologist," Fiona said.

"But I'm not!" Kitty said.

"You're supposed to pretend!"

"Oh," Kitty said.

Sophie patted her hand. "Maybe you should just listen at first, until you get the hang of it."

Kitty nodded glumly.

Sophie pushed her glasses up on her nose and went on. "Remember that we must scrape off only an eighth of an inch of dirt at a time and put it on the screens."

Sophie pointed a proud finger at the old pieces of screen she had placed over the openings of the white buckets.

"Why?" Kitty said.

Fiona gave a sigh that sounded as if it came from the pit of her stomach.

"So any pieces of artifacts will stay on the screen and the dirt will fall through," Sophie said.

Kitty craned her neck toward the buckets. "Those are going to be some pretty small articles."

"Artifacts!" Fiona practically screamed at her. Fiona's skin blushed toward the shade of a radish.

"I don't even think the dirt is going to go through holes that small," Kitty said.

Sophie had to admit she was probably right. "Okay," she said. "We won't use the screens. We'll just look at our dirt and if there's anything in it, we'll put it in this bucket, and we'll put the dirt in that bucket."

"Excellent plan, Doctor," Fiona said. "You amaze me with your expertise."

"Her what?" Kitty said.

Fiona sighed again. "Just pretend you know what I'm talking about, okay?"

They all went to work with their trowels, carefully scraping off soil with the sides of them, examining it closely for signs of armor or seventeenth century pottery, and dumping the dirt into the buckets.

After ten minutes, Dr. Demetria Diggerty's hand was starting to hurt, and Kitty was complaining that this was boring and that she was freezing. Even Artifacta Allen rocked back on her heels and said, "This is going to take forever, Soph—Doctor. I doubt that we're going to find any valuable evidence until we've dug down further."

"Yeah," Kitty said. "Don't you have any bigger shovels?"

That isn't the way they do it! Sophie wanted to say to them. But she knew if she did, Kitty would abandon the whole thing, and she and Fiona were determined to show Kitty that it was far better to be a Corn Flake than a Corn Pop.

She adjusted her Winnie-the-Pooh ball cap—the closest thing she could find to those hats the archaeologists at Jamestown were wearing—and nodded slowly.

"Agreed," she said. "Let's dig down two feet before we start sifting again."

"I would suggest three," Fiona said.

Kitty didn't say anything. She was already coming out of the garage dragging three shovels.

So they went to work again, talking as much like archaeologists as they could and hauling out huge shovelfuls of dirt and piling it against the fence. It turned out to be a lot more fun than scraping off tiny bits at a time, and even when it started to drizzle and Sophie had to wipe off her glasses every few minutes, they kept on; "spirits high!" as Fiona put it. In spite of her whining that it was time to get the camera out, Kitty got into the project too.

"I wanna be the first one to have my shovel hit the buried treasure chest," she said.

Both Fiona and Sophie stopped and stared at her.

"It's not that kind of treasure we're looking for," Sophie said.

"Then what is it?" Kitty said.

"Don't you remember, Madam Munford?" Fiona said between her teeth. "We are searching for small things that will help us understand the way the people before us lived."

Kitty poked her shovel back into the now very wet dirt. "I think they left a treasure chest," she said, and kept digging.

Dr. Demetria Diggerty smiled to herself. Perhaps she didn't have the brightest assistant in the field, but at least she was enthusiastic. By the time the camera crew arrived to film their progress, Madam Munford would be as professional as she and Artifacta were. She lifted her head from her digging to tell them both how much she appreciated their hard-working attitudes—and found herself looking right up into Daddy's scarlet face.

"Sophie—what in the world are you THINKING?"

Kitty whimpered, dropped her shovel with a splash into the hole, and took off toward the house, crying, "I have to call my mom. I have to go home!"

Fiona, on the other hand, leaned on her shovel and wafted an arm over their handiwork. "This is an archaeological dig," she said.

"No," Daddy said. "This is a mess. Sophie—you know what it took for your mother and me to put this yard in last summer— and here you are digging it up! What were you thinking?"

"I was thinking we would find some artifacts," Sophie said.

"And I'M thinking you're going to find the sprinkler system and chop a hole in a line!"

"We would know a sprinkler pipe wasn't an artifact, Mr. LaCroix," Fiona said. "We're professionals."

"Fiona," Daddy said, with his eyes still boring into Sophie, "go call your Boppa to come pick you up."

"Right now?" Fiona said.

"Go, Artifacta," Sophie said. "I will contact you later."

"Don't count on it, 'Artifacta'", Daddy said as Fiona reluctantly put down her shovel and trudged toward the house. "Sophie is going to be out of the loop for a while."

Sophie could feel Dr. Demetria Diggerty fighting to take over, yearning to turn and call to her colleague, "Don't worry. I will find a way. We will not be kept from our duty to history"—but she strained to stay focused on Daddy. It sounded like she was in enough trouble already.

"Artifacta?" Daddy said. "Never mind." He ran a hand over his hair as he looked down at the hole they'd been so proud of a few minutes before. His eyes were still blazing.

"I can't believe you did this," he said. "Is all that therapy doing any good at all?"

"Yes," Sophie said. "I'm making good grades. I have friends now—"

"You have friends, all right. Friends that aren't any more responsible than you are." Daddy snatched Sophie's shovel from her and picked up the other two with one hand. She could see the muscles in his jaw going into spasms. He looked over at the pile of dirt that had now turned to mud against the fence, and groaned.

"All right, here's the deal," he said. "It looks to me like you need some time apart from your 'friends' so you can think about your responsibilities. One week—"

A whole WEEK? Just for a hole? "No phone, no email, no TV, no camera."

"Can't I just fill in the hole and let that be my punishment?" Sophie said.

"Go to your room, Sophie," Daddy said, "before I say something we'll both regret."

Dr. Demetria Diggerty stormed to her living quarters, her dignity dashed and her project in ruins. But as she slammed her door behind her and hurled herself across her cot, she swore with her fists doubled that even the evil Enemy of History, Master LaCroix, would not stand in her way.

But that didn't help much. Sophie sat up on her bed and hugged a purple pillow against her chest.

Jesus, she thought. *I'm supposed to imagine Jesus when I get mad—not Dr. Diggerty.*

She closed her eyes and tried to picture the kind man who always seemed to understand. She could almost see him—but not quite. His edges were fuzzy this time.

Sophie squeezed her eyes shut tighter and tried some more. *I know you love me, Jesus. There aren't any ifs anymore. I know you're there—*

But she couldn't quite see his face in her mind. It was a good thing, she decided, that the next day was a Dr. Peter day.

Daddy told her that night, when he came in to get the camera, that he couldn't keep her from being with her friends at school, but he "advised her" to spend any of her free time there working on her studies and "getting serious." She didn't remind him that there wasn't much point in getting good grades if she didn't get to have her camera anyway. She decided it would be better to discuss that with Dr. Peter.

So all day long she suffered through Kitty's tearful looks and Fiona's notes asking her why she didn't stage a mutiny on her father, which was what SHE would do. Finally, school was over and Mama picked her up to take her to Hampton for her appointment.

At first they rode in stiff silence, as if the air between them had been spray starched. All Sophie could think about was that if Mama was going to go along with this heinous punishment, she couldn't confide in her. She didn't know WHAT Mama was thinking.

"Do you want to talk about it?" Mama said finally.

"No, thank you," Sophie said.

But she did squirm in her seat belt and say, "I'm sorry if it upset you that I dug a hole in the yard. I didn't think you would mind."

"We don't always know what people would and wouldn't mind about what belongs to them," Mama said. "That's why we ask first."

But you weren't there! Sophie wanted to say. *You were off doing something for Lacie. Like usual.*

Sophie even turned to her to maybe say SOME of that, but Mama looked as if she were already thinking about something else. Something that had nothing to do with her.

The minute Mama pulled up to the clinic, Sophie was out of the Suburban and inside Dr. Peter's office. As always, he was waiting for her at the front counter with a "Sophie-Lophie-Loodle! Good to see you!"

"We need to talk," she said.

"Of course," he said. His face grew serious and his blue eyes stopped twinkling behind his glasses. "That's what I'm here for."

Sophie climbed up onto the window seat in Dr. Peter's office and grabbed one of the face pillows to crunch against her. She could feel a stuffed nose pressing into her chest, and she plucked angrily at an ear that poked out the side.

"Okay, Loodle," Dr. Peter said when he was settled at the other end of the seat. "Give me the goods."

She did, pouring out everything, good and evil. Aunt Bailey and Uncle Preston. Jamestown. Dr. Demetria Diggerty. Bra shopping. And, of course, the hideous groundation punishment.

"And you know what's the absolute worst?" she said when she had come to the end.

Dr. Peter shook his head of short, curly, reddish brown hair. He was looking at her soberly.

"I tried to imagine Jesus so I could ask for help—and then I was gonna wait for it, like you taught me—only it didn't work."

"You didn't get the help yet?"

"No! I couldn't even imagine his face!" Sophie swallowed hard. "I needed to see his eyes in my mind."

"And it upset you that you couldn't."

Sophie nodded. "Are you sure he's really always there? He doesn't get busy with somebody else's stuff?"

"I'm absolutely sure. That's the cool thing about Jesus: with him, it's always all about you and him, just like it's all about me and him, and all about whoever and him."

"Then where is he?" Sophie said.

Dr. Peter pressed his hand against his chest. "He's in there. We know that for sure, because you always fill up your space with the things that God loves."

"Then I guess I had some No-God space last night," Sophie said.

The serious face broke into a crinkly road map of smiling lines. "I like that, Loodle. There can be only two types of space within a person, God and No-God. Where we want to stay is our choice."

"I want to stay in God-space! Only it's hard when I'm mad."

"Understood," Dr. Peter said. "But you can stay in God-space if you know more about Jesus—what he was like on earth and still is in Spirit. Hey—" His eyes sparked to life again. "You want to do a little archaeology into Jesus' childhood?"

Sophie squinted at him through her glasses. "Wouldn't we have to go to Nazareth to do that?"

"Nope—although wouldn't we have a blast?"

Sophie had to agree that they would. In fact, she had to work hard for a minute to keep Dr. Demetria Diggerty from taking completely over and planning the trip.

"No, our best site for digging," Dr. Peter went on, "is in the gospel of Luke. I'm going to write down some Bible verses for you to read and picture in your mind. It sounds like you're going to have plenty of time for that this week."

Sophie scowled. "I sure hope this works," she said. "'Cause I'm tired of getting mad all the time."

Dr. Peter let a silence fall, though it wasn't a starched-up one like she had sat through with Mama in the car. While he was writing on a piece of paper with a purple Sharpie, Sophie sighed back into the cushions and let her thoughts settle down.

"Tell me something, Loodle," Dr. Peter said finally. His voice was soft. "What do you want most in the world right now, right this very second?"

Sophie didn't even have to think about it. "I want my father to stand up for me, just once," she said. "Instead of always saying everything that happens is my fault and telling me what I should have done different."

Dr. Peter nodded as he handed her the paper. "It's time to dig in with God then, Loodle. I think this is going to help you meet the challenge."

Dig in. Meet a challenge.

Now THOSE sounded like words for Dr. Demetria Diggerty. Sophie took the paper and gave Dr. Peter a promise nod.

Five

🌿 ✳ ❋

Sophie wanted to go straight up to her room when they got home and start digging into Jesus' past. But Mama made her come to the table for chicken casserole, which felt like cardboard in her mouth as she listened to Lacie go on and on about—what else?—Aunt Bailey and how she and Lacie had emailed each other six times already.

"Did you know she played sports in middle school and high school too, just like me?" Lacie said.

"Really?" Daddy said. "My brother never mentioned that to me."

"She did," Lacie said. "And she was good—especially in basketball—"

"Well, isn't that special?" Mama pushed back her chair and picked up the still-almost-full muffin basket. "We need more bread," she said, and she disappeared into the kitchen.

"I didn't even get one yet!" Zeke wailed.

Sophie stuck hers on his plate.

"Is Mom still mad at you because Aunt Bailey and Uncle Preston came here for Thanksgiving instead of us going to see Grandpa?" Lacie said to Daddy.

"Where did you get that idea?" Daddy said. He touched Lacie lightly on the nose and added, "Pass the salad dressing, would you?"

"Oh, come on," Lacie said. "She's been all tense since before they even came. All snappin' at me." Lacie lowered her voice as if she and Daddy were in on some kind of conspiracy. "I think she's a little jealous because Aunt Bailey and I got along so good."

Oh, for Pete's sake! Sophie thought. *Mama isn't some Corn Pop. Who CARES about Aunt Bailey?*

SHE certainly didn't. What she cared about was getting up to her room so she could start digging. She stuffed a couple of forkfuls of asparagus into her mouth, chewed furiously, and said, with her cheeks still packed, "I'm full. Can I be excused?"

Daddy nodded absently. He looked like what Lacie was saying was the most fascinating thing since the sports page.

Up in her room, Sophie pulled her Bible off the shelf and then settled herself precisely on her bed. This was going to be like using documental evidence, so she carefully arranged a sharpened pencil, with only a few teeth marks in it, her ideas notebook turned to a fresh page and, after some thought, her magnifying glass, just in case she needed to look VERY closely.

Then, with the anticipation of a new discovery coursing through her veins, Dr. Demetria Diggerty turned each page as if it were a fine piece of onion skin, until she reached the gospel of Luke, chapter 2, verse 41. She held her breath—

Sophie stopped, breath still sucked in. Maybe she shouldn't dig as Dr. Diggerty.

If it was really going to help with the Daddy problem, she should probably do this as Sophie.

Still, she reached up on the headboard for her cap and set it in archaeological position on her head before she began to read.

It was the story about Jesus at age twelve going with his parents to Jerusalem for the Feast of the Passover. Sophie had heard the story before—probably about a bajillion times in Sunday school—but this time she tried to picture it as she read.

She could see Jesus finding the teachers in their long beards and fancy robes, sitting around on the stone floors of the magnificent temple. Jesus hanging out with them instead of going out partying with everyone else. And asking questions that echoed through the halls, impressing the sandals off of all the learned men.

She paused for a long time over the line, *Everyone who heard him was amazed at his understanding and his answers.*

"That's what I'M talkin' about," Sophie whispered.

She dug back in and read more and imagined Mary and Joseph bursting into the temple all scarlet-faced and chewing Jesus out because he had worried them sick. She could almost hear Mary saying that they had been looking all over for him—only it sounded more like Daddy's voice in her mind. Jesus' voice was clear and strong as he asked them why they were even worried about him when they should have known he'd be in his Father's house.

And then she got to the line that left no space for anything else: *But they did not understand what he was saying to them.*

Sophie closed the Bible and hugged it to her chest, her eyes closed so the picture of a frustrated twelve-year-old Jesus wouldn't go away. She imagined it for a long time—his confusion that they didn't know who he really was, the stirrings of anger he must have felt because they were mad at him for doing something that was only wrong to THEM. Again and again she could almost see his face as his parents looked at him, shaking their heads. *They did not understand what he was saying to them.*

"Wow," Sophie whispered. "I think I know exactly how you felt."

There was a tap on the door, and there was no time for Sophie to grab for her backpack and get out her homework before it opened and Mama came in. Sophie knew her face was as give-away guilty as Zeke's was whenever Mama caught him spitting mouthfuls of broccoli into his napkin.

"I'm starting my homework," Sophie said.

Mama cocked her head as she sat down on the end of Sophie's bed. "Did you think I was going to yell at you or something?"

"I was doing something else besides homework—well, SCHOOL homework."

"Honey," Mama said, "I would never scold you for reading the Bible! Give me a big ol' break!"

Sophie nodded and hoped Mama wasn't reading her mind. She was still thinking, *They did not understand* ...

"I've come to make you an offer," Mama said. "I've talked this over with your father and he has given his okay IF you still get your schoolwork done."

"He's going to let me fill in the hole instead of being grounded!" Sophie said.

Mama just blinked. "No," she said. "He's already filled in the hole. And he wasn't happy about it."

"Oh," Sophie said. No telling how much valuable physical evidence he covered back up.

"Here is the deal," Mama said. "If you want to pursue your archaeology, you can start by digging in the attic while you're grounded. You know Uncle Preston brought that big trunk with him from Great-Grandma LaCroix's estate, and I haven't even opened it yet." Her eyebrows twitched. "He and Aunt Bailey said they don't want any of that 'old junk,' and I don't have time to go through it right now, so why don't you have a go at it? Maybe you could make me a detailed list of the contents. How would that be?"

"That would be incredible!" Sophie said.

"Just do it AFTER your homework is done. Maybe you shouldn't even think about doing it until this weekend. I just wanted to tell you now so you'll have something to look forward to."

Sophie threw her arms around Mama's neck—even though she wasn't sure that was something Dr. Demetria Diggerty would do.

"You are the best mom," she said.

"It's nice to hear that Tinker Bell laugh again, Dream Girl," Mama said.

When she was gone, Sophie sank back into her pillows and gazed up at her ceiling, dotted with fluorescent stars. She didn't really see them, though. She saw herself in the attic, an important-looking clipboard on her arm, peering through a magnifying glass at a piece of china so thin and old it had to go back as far as—maybe the 1950s or something ...

And then she imagined the kind eyes of Jesus, and she decided she was back in God-space.

But it was hard to stay there for the whole next three days. Mama had been right that there would be no time to go into the attic until the weekend. In the meantime, although she worked hard to keep up with her homework, it was hard without Fiona to encourage her on the phone, or Kitty to keep her spirits up with the cheesy jokes she told her on the phone when she WASN'T grounded.

Besides, being home ALL the time meant that the things that drove her nuts were constantly all around her.

Lacie was "tearing it up" in basketball, as Daddy put it. When she was chosen captain of the team, Daddy brought home a cake with a miniature basketball hoop actually standing up on it. Zeke thought that was the coolest thing ever. Sophie felt shoved out.

Zeke, of course, was adorable, and she loved reading to him and playing games with him and his little plastic cars. But the day he dismantled the coffee maker, she was flabbergasted that HE didn't get grounded. He got a thirty-minute time-out, and Daddy explained to him how he could have hurt himself with the electricity—blah, blah, blah—but there was nowhere near the upheaval that had occurred when she dug one little hole in the backyard. She didn't want to resent her little brother, but she didn't feel as much like playing with him after that.

It was even hard with Mama. It wasn't that she was getting all "yelly" as Zeke would call it. In fact, she just kept being quieter and quieter, and once Sophie thought she heard her crying in the night when she got up to go to the bathroom. Back in bed, Sophie got Jesus in her mind and begged him to fix whatever was wrong with her mom.

It felt so much better to be in God-space for those few moments that Sophie decided to try harder to stay there. When Fiona and Kitty complained during lunch the next day about Sophie's groundation, Sophie told them the story about Jesus, and how she could relate to that because, like his parents, hers didn't understand her purpose either.

"Huh," Fiona said. "When it comes to LACIE'S purpose, your father is all over it."

That was true, and it sent Sophie scurrying to Dr. Diggerty, presenting an antique basketball hoop that she had pulled out of the rubble to the evil Master LaCroix, Enemy of History.

"Of what use is a rusty old piece of sports equipment?" he said to her. "I can buy hundreds of new ones. I see no further need for your services." Dr. Diggerty did not even lower her head. She knew he simply did not understand. She would fight for her career. She would fight to look though the lenses of the past . . .

She felt a hard nudge in her ribs, and she jerked her head around.

Harley was poking her. "She wants to say somethin' to ya," she said.

Sophie looked across the table at Maggie. Her face was set like cement.

"Maggie!" Sophie said. "You're sitting with us!"

"I'm only here to tell you something important." Maggie said.

"So dish," Fiona said. She leaned in on her elbow, chin in hand.

Maggie slanted her eyes at the Wheaties and the Corn Flakes, and then she pointed her eyes at Sophie. "There's a rumor going around about you."

"Let me guess who's spreading it," Fiona said. She glared past Maggie at the Corn Pops, who currently had their heads all bent over something on their table.

"That's right," Maggie said.

"I bet it's bad if they're spreading it," Kitty said. "No, I KNOW it's bad!"

"You know what?" Sophie said to Maggie. "I don't want to hear it."

Maggie gave her an open-eyed look. "You don't?"

"Nope. If it's a rumor, then it isn't true, so what do I care?"

"Sophie's right," Fiona said. She folded her arms across her chest. "It stops here."

"That's fine with me," Maggie said. She shoved her chair back and slung her lunch bag strap over her shoulder. "I just thought you'd want to know."

"Thanks," Sophie said.

"But no thanks," Fiona said.

Sophie felt a pang as Maggie trudged heavily away. Maybe if she had listened to what Maggie had to say, she would have stayed and they could have made things up to her—

But Harley banged her on the back and told her she rocked, and Sophie decided maybe that was just as good. Meanwhile, Kitty was gazing, wide-eyed, at Fiona.

"What?" Fiona said. "Do I have a booger hanging out of my nose or something?"

"You stood up for Sophie," Kitty said.

"Of course I did. We're Corn Flakes. We do that for each other."

"Oh," Kitty said.

That was Friday, the last school day before Sophie's grounding period was over.

"I'm gonna be so glad when Monday comes," Fiona told her as they were cramming their books into their lockers after school. "If we don't start playing again, I think I'm going to go into cardiac arrest."

Sophie knew that had something to do with dying, which didn't cheer her up much. "We only get to play if I improve at least a point in everything on my progress report Monday."

"You're going to, so quit stressing out. We need to be thinking about WHAT we're going to play—"

But Sophie suddenly had it. She had just emptied her backpack into her locker—because there was no homework over the weekend. That meant she could devote all her time to the excavation of the attic. What if—

"We could all three of us do our archaeology in my attic!" Sophie said. "This could be so cool—and my mother already said it was okay so we don't have to worry about my father yelling at us—well, me."

"Fabulous," Fiona said. Her eyes took on her deep, intrigued look. "You could develop a plan over the weekend so we can start Monday—"

"No—Tuesday. I have to wait 'til my dad gets home Monday to get off groundation."

"Okay—Tuesday. I'm going to work on Boppa for some actual hard hats like the archaeologists wear. He'll want to get out of the house anyway. We have a new nanny for Rory and Isabella, and she has so many rules, she's even starting to tell Boppa what to do!"

Boppa was Fiona's grandfather, who was like a mom and a dad to Fiona and her little brother and sister because her parents were WAY busy people and weren't around much. Sophie was sure Fiona would show up with something close to real-thing hats. Boppa didn't say no to her very often.

So Sophie went home that day with a lighter heart, and she started in on the attic right away, ball cap on backwards and notebook in hand. It wasn't an actual clipboard, but a pencil tucked behind her ear made her feel more professional.

Grandma Too was the name Lacie had given their great-grandma as a little kid when she realized she had a grandma—their father's mom—and HER mother was another grandma too.

Once Sophie opened Grandma Too's trunk, the rest of the world ceased to exist. Inside were treasures like she never would have found in the backyard, she was sure, and her disappointment at not being able to use the trenching technique slowly faded.

There was a pair of Grandma Too's underwear, paper-thin and yellowed and as big as the shorts Lacie wore to play basketball in. The tag pinned to them with a rusty safety pin said she had worn them on her wedding day, in 1939.

"Very significant," Sophie said, and jotted that down in her notebook.

There were dried flowers, now in confetti flakes, from Too's bridal bouquet, and a gavel from when she was president of the Ladies' Auxiliary. Sophie wasn't sure what that was, but it was engraved in the brass plate which she examined with her magnifying glass, so it must be historically important.

"This is the best," she murmured to herself. "The best, the best, the best."

She spent all of Friday evening going through the trunk, and she was up first thing Saturday, even before Zeke, and got back at it again. There was much work to be done.

But Dr. Demetria Diggerty was no stranger to hard work and long hours. These precious treasures had been hidden away for far too long, by those misers of historical knowledge, Preston and Bailey McEvil. "I will dig until I drop," Dr. Diggerty said. "I will not stop until I have discovered everything about the life of this amazing woman of another time and place—"

"Daddy, do you hear her talking to herself?"

Sophie jumped and looked around. Was somebody else in the attic with her? Like Lacie?

It took Sophie a minute to realize that Lacie's voice, and then Daddy's, were coming through the floor. Of course. This part of the attic was right above Lacie's room.

Sophie—Dr. Diggerty—tried to return to her work, but it was as if she were being pulled by the ear to listen to them.

"I hear her," Daddy said. "But I think that's going to stop soon. She's starting to change."

"Right," Lacie said.

"And I think it's because of you, Lace."

"Are you kidding? Daddy, she won't listen to a thing I say."

Sophie heard the chair creak, and she knew Daddy was sitting down on the corner of it.

"You might not think she's listening, but she's watching you," Daddy said. "That's one of the reasons I grounded her, so she'd be around you more often. You're a good role model for her."

"Thanks," Lacie said.

You have to be KIDDING! Sophie thought.

"You're always my go-to guy," Daddy said. "I know I can count on you."

As the chair creaked again and Lacie's door opened and closed, Sophie put her face into the pile of linens she'd pulled out of Grandma Too's trunk and decided this must be what it felt like to be an orphan.

I really, really know how you felt, Jesus, she thought with her eyes squeezed tight. *Because now I know how MUCH my father doesn't understand.*

Six

Sophie worked in Dr. Demetria Diggerty's world for the rest of the weekend.

When she couldn't be in the attic—like when they went to church and when Daddy took them all out to the Crab Cake House—she tried to imagine Jesus and how HE felt when HIS father didn't get HIM either. All of that kept her from remembering what Daddy had said—about Lacie being a role model for her—and from worrying about whether she was going to improve on her progress report. She still didn't know what "cardiac arrest" was, but she was sure that she, like Fiona, was going to have it if she didn't get to start making films with the Corn Flakes again.

Monday, when Sophie saw the last grade of the last class, she decided that Jesus had been listening.

"What's the verdict?" Fiona whispered to her while their math and science teacher, Mrs. Utley, was passing out the rest of the progress reports.

Sophie gave her a slow smile. "Drum roll, please," she said.

Fiona nodded at Kitty, who giggled and rapped her hands several times on her desktop.

"Language Arts—up by three points."

"And?"

"Social Studies—up by FIVE points. That's because I did extra credit after I went to Jamestown . . ."

"Go ON, already!"

"Computers—up by one and a half points. Same with health."

"Whew—close one."

"Math—up by three points."

Kitty and Fiona didn't say anything this time. They seemed to be holding the same breath as they watched Sophie's lips.

"And science—up by one half of a point."

"No!" the Corn Flakes said together.

"You're right. I'm kidding," said Sophie. "Up by one point. One wonderful point!"

The three of them started to shout a collective "Yes!", but that drew a wiggle from one of Mrs. Utley's soft chins, so they settled for their secret pinkie handshake, done in clandestine fashion between the desks.

From across the room, Sophie caught Maggie watching them, and for a second Sophie thought she looked a little wishful. But as soon as her eyes met Maggie's, she busied herself with packing up her backpack. *That was still a thing that had to be fixed,* Sophie thought. *But right now—*

Right now it was time to celebrate. Well, almost. She still had to wait until Daddy got home from work, and when he didn't arrive until almost 6:30, she was convinced he was stalling on purpose. By the time he came in the back door, she was pacing a path in the kitchen floor. The progress report was in his hand before Zeke could crawl up his leg or Lacie could get to him with her new free-throw average. They didn't even get to the kitchen.

"Don't worry—it's good," Sophie said as she watched Daddy's eyes sweep the page.

"You barely scraped by with getting the one-point improvement in a couple of subjects," he said. "But you met the requirements. I guess I have to give that camera back to you."

"And I'm off groundation, right?" Sophie said.

Daddy took his time putting his briefcase down and peeling off his jacket. He sure looked to Sophie as if he wanted to say no.

At last he sat down on a stool at the snack bar, so that at least he wasn't looking at her from his towering height. "Do you think you've learned something from being grounded?" he said.

"Yes," Sophie said.

"What?"

"That I shouldn't mess with other people's stuff—like their lawn—without asking first."

"That's it?"

Sophie blinked. "Is there supposed to be more?"

"Seems like it to me," Daddy said.

Actually, there WAS more in Sophie's mind, but she wasn't sure Daddy would want to hear it. She closed her eyes and tried to imagine Jesus, explaining HIS purpose to HIS parents. Maybe there was a way . . .

Passing up *I learned that you really do want me to be a clone of Lacie*, Sophie took a deep breath and said, "I learned that you want me to be a team player and do everything the way everybody else in the family does it."

Daddy started to nod, but then he didn't. His black eyebrows bunched together over his nose. "Anything else?"

"That's what I learned from YOU," she said.

Daddy leaned forward, like he was suddenly very interested. "So you learned some things from somebody else through all this?" he said.

Sophie almost nodded. She almost told him about the Jesus-story Dr. Peter had given her. She almost did. Until she remembered that conversation she'd heard through the attic floor.

He's thinking I learned something from Lacie, she thought. *No way. That is just—that's heinous!*

Daddy was still looking at her, his blue eyes waiting.

"I learned from Mama," she said, "that you don't have to dig holes in other people's property to be an archaeologist. I'm having great success in the attic."

It was as if someone had ripped a mask off of Daddy and left him with a totally different face. He sat back on the stool and rubbed his palms up and down his thighs. Sophie waited, holding her breath.

"Okay. You're free," he said, "but just—just think before you do things from now on, all right?"

Think like Lacie, you mean! Sophie wanted to cry out at him. But there was still one more question she wanted to ask, and she couldn't do anything to jeopardize the answer being YES.

"So is it okay if Kitty and Fiona come over and film in the attic with me tomorrow after school?" she said.

"Tomorrow is a Dr. Peter day," Mama said from behind them.

Sophie didn't know when she had slipped in. She was carrying a box with various Christmas decorations poking out the top.

"But I don't see why they can't come Wednesday," Mama said. "I'll have all the Christmas stuff out of the attic by then so I won't be in your way."

"We definitely wouldn't want to get in your way," Daddy said to Sophie.

"Hello!" Mama said.

Sophie looked quickly at her. The drawstring mouth was pulled so tight, she wasn't sure how Mama had gotten even that much out.

"Sorry—just messing around," Daddy said. He took the box from Mama. "Where do you want this?"

She jerked her curls toward the kitchen table.

"Sure, bring in the Dream Team," Daddy said over his shoulder to Sophie. "Just don't—"

"I know," Sophie said. "I'll be aware of my surroundings and I won't lose touch with the real world and I'll be a team player and I won't think everything is always all about me. Can I go to my room now?"

"Absolutely," Mama said.

As she made for the stairs, Sophie heard Daddy say, "What was that all about?"

She didn't hear what Mama said. She wasn't sure she wanted to.

It was still disappointing that Daddy was probably never going to stand behind her the way she wanted him to. But the next day at lunch as she looked at the happy cluster of girls at her table—Harley and Gill and Vette and Nikki and Kitty and Fiona—she decided she had plenty of other people to do that, and she felt her wisp of a smile forming.

It got bigger when Maggie plunked herself down across from her.

"You're here!" Sophie said.

"I just have a question for you," she said.

"Yes, you can still be a Corn Flake girl—anytime you want."

Maggie rolled her eyes. "You can give that up," she said. "It's a different question."

"So stop loitering around it and ask it," Fiona said.

"Only Sophie can answer it," Maggie said, every word heavy.

"Which she can only do if you ASK IT!" Fiona said.

Maggie ignored her. Her dark eyes were on Sophie. "Is it true that you're going to a psychiatrist?"

Sophie's tongue turned to stone right in her mouth. That was something Kitty and Fiona already knew, and it was no big deal to them. But Harley and Gill and the twins didn't know about it. What were they going to think?

Sophie could feel her cheeks burning, and it was all she could do not to lower her head and pull her long hair over her face. But she didn't know why, not really. It had always been so easy to just be honest about things. Now she wasn't sure she could even get her tongue moving.

"That is SO nobody's business but Sophie's!" Fiona said.

"YOU know, though, don't you?" Maggie said to her.

"Only because she wanted to tell me—not because I plopped myself in the middle of her business and asked her!"

Gill put her mouth close to Sophie's ear. "Harley wants to know if you want her to kick Maggie's tail."

"No!" Sophie said. It was suddenly enough that they were sticking up for her. She straightened her shoulders. "I don't go to a psychiatrist," she said.

"See!" Gill said.

"I go to a child psychologist. He helps me figure things out so I can get better grades and have friends and understand about God."

"Oh," Maggie said. The expression on her face didn't change from its set-in-concrete stare. "So are you crazy or not?"

"No, she's not crazy!" Fiona said. "Does she ACT like she's crazy?"

Maggie shrugged. "Sometimes. When she's all pretending and stuff—it's like it's real to her."

"And this is a problem because?" Fiona said.

Maggie gave a final shrug and got up. "I was just asking," she said.

She lumbered off toward the trashcans.

"Thanks, y'all," Sophie said.

"Of course," Fiona said. And then she switched the subject to what everybody was asking to get for Christmas.

Sophie couldn't wait to get settled in on the window seat that afternoon to tell Dr. Peter what she'd learned from the Bible verses and how it was working. She didn't even have to hug a face pillow while she was talking.

But to her surprise, he picked one up and toyed with its fuzzy eyebrows before he said, "So did you read the rest of it, Loodle?"

"There was more?"

"I love what you got out of that part." Dr. Peter wrinkled his nose so his glasses scooted up. "But what do you say we dig a little deeper, together? I have a surprise for you."

Sophie could feel her smile spreading practically to her earlobes as Dr. Peter reached behind him and pulled out two helmets. They looked just like what explorers wore in those old movies about going on safaris and stuff. She had watched the animated version of *Tarzan* with Zeke enough times to recognize them immediately.

"Are these for us?" she said. She could hear her voice going up into its high-pitched squeal.

"A helmet for each of us," Dr. Peter said. He handed Sophie one and perched the other on top of his gel-stiff curls. "Because you never know what kind of jungle we might get into."

Sophie tucked her hair up into hers, and although it came down to the tip of her nose and she had to tilt her head to see, she felt more like Dr. Demetria Diggerty than ever. But she concentrated on staying in Sophie-Land.

"All right, fellow explorer." Dr. Peter pulled a Bible and a magnifying glass out of a daypack on the floor. "Just in case," he said. "Now, Luke two, verse fifty-one."

"I'll dig for it," Sophie said. She ruffled through the pages and located their excavation site. But she handed it back to Dr. Peter for the actual reading, so she could close her eyes and imagine.

"'Then he went down to Nazareth with them,'" Dr. Peter read. "'Them' would be his parents."

"I can see them," Sophie said. She nodded, eyes still closed. "Dig on."

"'Then he went down to Nazareth with them, and was obedient to them. But his mother treasured all these things in her heart. And Jesus grew in wisdom and stature, and in favor with God and men.'"

"What about his father?" Sophie said.

"It doesn't say anything about his father," Dr. Peter said.

"Okay. Go on."

"That's it."

Sophie opened her eyes. "But what happens after that?"

"The next time we see Jesus is when he's about thirty and he gets baptized by John the Baptist."

"Oh." Sophie could feel her eyebrows twisting. "So he didn't ever make his parents understand? He just had to find other people who did? And he didn't find them until he was THIRTY?"

Dr. Peter pulled out the magnifying glass and applied it to the page, brow furrowed. When he looked up at Sophie, he shook his head. "That's not what I see here."

"What do you see?" Sophie said.

Dr. Peter nodded for her to look on with him as he traced the lines in Luke with his finger. "Looks to me like he went home with his parents and obeyed them. And that's how he grew in wisdom and stature and favor with God and men. Women too, I'm sure."

"What's 'stature'?" Sophie said.

"Height."

"Oh, well, forget that," Sophie said. "I'm underdeveloped." She looked at him from under the brim of her helmet. "Does this mean if I obey my parents I'll actually grow? Maybe need a bra someday?"

She could see that Dr. Peter was trying to smother a smile. "No, I think God's in charge of that," he said.

Sophie looked at the Bible again, and she could feel herself pulling back.

"Talk to me, Loodle," Dr. Peter said.

"I don't think I like this part," Sophie said. "It's like it's saying I have to obey my parents even if they—well, Daddy—don't even understand me."

"That's what Jesus did." Dr. Peter pulled a canteen out of the daypack and offered it to her. "Drink?"

Sophie shook her head. As Fiona would have said, she was completely despondent.

Dr. Peter took a few chugs out of the canteen and wiped his lips with the back of his hand, just like a true explorer, but there was no magic in it for Sophie.

"You're not a happy archaeologist right now," Dr. Peter said.

Sophie pulled off her helmet and handed it to him. "I don't think I want to dig anymore," she said. "Not if this is what I'm going to find out."

Dr. Peter looked her right in the eyes.

"Sometimes I don't like what Jesus is trying to tell me the first time I read it, either," he said. "But if I follow it, it never fails me."

Sophie didn't answer.

"Have I ever steered you wrong, Loodle?" he said.

"No," Sophie said.

"So you'll try it? After all, you and Jesus have a lot in common."

Sophie glared at the Bible. "I wish it gave more details about HOW he did it."

Dr. Peter's eyes twinkled. "Those you'll have to get from him," he said. "So keep on digging."

Seven

Sophie kept telling herself that she HAD to do it—that she HAD to obey everything Mama and Daddy said, even if they, or at least Daddy, WERE trying to turn her into Lacie.

She prayed with her eyes scrunched shut that Daddy wouldn't decide to make her go out for basketball or require her to get straight A's. Or worse: make her be friends with Aunt Bailey and wear a padded bra.

That was why it was SO easy to throw herself completely into the excavation of the attic when Wednesday afternoon finally came and she and Fiona and Kitty were gathered in front of Grandma Too's trunk.

They had taken Kitty's suggestion and dressed up like archaeologists. Kitty might not have been the best pretender in the Corn Flakes, but she had the best costume.

While Sophie and Fiona were basically in khaki shorts and white T-shirts and floppy hats (Boppa had obviously not forked over for genuine digging hats), Kitty looked as if she could go to work at Jamestown that very minute.

She had on khaki cargo pants with lots of pockets, and a bright red hard hat—a real one—and hiking boots. The best part was the canvas vest with zippered pockets that held everything, including a neat little pad, a pencil, and a pair of glasses with the magnifiers attached to them.

"Where did you get all this cool stuff?" Fiona said.

"My daddy took me shopping," she said. "We went to that sporting goods store at the mall."

"Wow," Sophie said. She couldn't keep the envy out of her voice.

"Even my Boppa doesn't spoil me that much," Fiona said.

"This isn't spoiling," Kitty said. "He hardly ever buys any of us anything unless it's Christmas or our birthday."

Sophie could understand that. There were six girls in Kitty's family.

"He just said he's glad to see me do something with people besides Julia and them," Kitty said, "because all they ever did was put on makeup and call boys and watch PG-13 movies. And make me cry."

"Are you glad you're a Corn Flake now?" Sophie said.

"You guys don't make me cry," Kitty said.

Sophie decided that was good enough for now. They had important work to do.

First Sophie showed them all the things she had pulled out of Grandma Too's trunk and put on her list. Fiona nodded approvingly.

They decided that Grandma Too had had an extraordinary life — though Kitty still didn't understand why a woman would get married in boxer shorts — and that they wanted to know more about her descendants.

"How do we do that?" Kitty said.

Fiona waved an arm over the plastic containers she'd been peeking into. "It's all right here," she said. "In all these photo albums and scrapbooks."

Kitty wrinkled her nose. "That sounds boring to me."

"An archaeologist is never bored," Artifacta informed her. "Even with the most tedious work."

"Huh," said Madam Munford.

"I know what," Sophie said quickly. Then she cleared her throat and adjusted her glasses. "Madam Munford, I suggest that you learn to operate the video camera so that you can record the amazing discoveries as we make them."

"Cool!" Kitty said.

"Do archaeologists say 'cool'?" Fiona said.

"Oh, yes," Sophie said. It was clear they weren't going to transform Kitty into Madam Munford in just one digging session.

So as Kitty examined the camera and climbed all over the attic like a spider monkey taking shots of them, Dr. Demetria Diggerty and Artifacta Allen pored over the infant pictures of dozens of LaCroixs and Castilles, which had been Mama's last name before she married Daddy.

They made a packet for each one and created a sheet to go with the baby picture, on which they described how they thought that child had turned out, based on the documental evidence they were finding. They also lapsed into Sophie and Fiona now and then to try to guess who the babies were before they turned the photos over to read the names on the back.

It took them until late Saturday to go through all the plastic containers, as well as Grandma Too's trunk. By then, they had thirty packets, on everyone from Grandma Too herself—born in 1916!—to Zeke, and every conceivable cousin, aunt, uncle, and grandparent in between.

As they held up their flashlights to gaze at their work—and Kitty got it all on film—something suddenly struck Sophie.

"Hey," she said. "We don't have a packet for me."

"You musta missed a box," Kitty said.

"No, we didn't," Fiona said in her Artifacta voice. "Our work has been very thorough."

Sophie nodded—as professionally as she could—but her Sophie-self was plunging into a strange place. She sat down on top of Grandma Too's trunk.

"I'm sure your stuff is around here someplace," Fiona said. "You all just moved last summer. Maybe it's in a box in the garage or something. Or maybe it got lost in the moving van." Fiona wiggled her eyebrows. "Maybe we should trace the path of the van and try to find it in a ditch along the road."

Sophie tried to smile, but even her mouth was sagging. It was as if she were seeing right in front of her what she felt so often in her house: that everybody counted but her.

"Hey, I know," Kitty said. She put down the camera and perched on one of the plastic containers. "Maybe you're adopted."

"What?" Fiona said. "I know we're supposed to examine every theory—but that's just—"

"My oldest sister was adopted," Kitty said. "And then, BAM, my parents had five kids of their own."

"No offense, Kitty," Fiona said. "But that is just ridiculous. Sophie's the middle kid. Why would her parents adopt another kid when they already had one, and then HAVE another one—"

Sophie was glad when Mama called up the steps that Boppa was there to pick up Fiona and Kitty. She was also glad that Mama and Daddy went to the NASA Christmas party that night, and Lacie was "babysitting," so Sophie could take her piece of pizza up to her room and not eat it in the kitchen.

She tried to dream up Dr. Demetria Diggerty and perhaps have her argue that there was no possible way Sophie was adopted. The physical evidence didn't point to that; people were always saying that she looked so much like Mama.

But Dr. Diggerty refused to cooperate, and Sophie knew she should go to Jesus.

He was kind of adopted, she thought. *God was in heaven and he lived with Mary and Joseph.*

But his mother—she was his birth mother. Every Christmas as far back as she could remember, she'd heard that story—how Mary gave birth to him in the manger. Somebody else didn't have him and then find other parents for him—

Sophie closed her eyes so tightly her forehead hurt. Jesus was there. His eyes were kind. But all she could think of him saying was, "Be obedient to your parents." And it sounded like Dr. Peter's voice.

She wished Dr. Peter were there right then. She had some questions for HIM:

Like—*Do I have to be obedient to people who aren't even my parents—who have been lying to me ever since I was a little kid—even though they're always telling ME I have to be honest? And I always AM!*

Sophie could hear Zeke and Lacie on the other side of the big square hallway in Zeke's room, where Lacie was reading Zeke the five hundredth book so he would go to sleep. She could picture them with their dark thick hair—not like her own wispy brown—and their sharp faces—not like her own elfin look. They were so much alike—and so much like Daddy—

Sophie suddenly bolted from the bed and ran to the corner of her room, where she wrapped her arms around herself and scrunched her eyes tighter and tried to cut off the thought that was filling her up: No wonder Daddy will stand up for Lacie and not me. She's his own flesh and blood. And I'm not.

Sophie knew she was in the land of No-God. And even the picture of Jesus' kind eyes couldn't seem to pull her out.

For the next several days, she pretended she wasn't in No-God Land, and the only way to do that was to spend every spare moment with the Corn Flakes, developing their babies' stories and finding more information. Fiona brought them a perfect notebook for all the packets. It was purple with plastic daisies and a tab that snapped shut. Sophie knew Boppa had bought it, and she tried not to wish that she could go live with HER grandfather. She really didn't know him—

And besides, if he's Mama's father, then he isn't my flesh and blood—and Grandma Too wasn't either—

That hurt so much in the middle of her chest, Sophie dove back into their project with double-deep energy.

One of the things that WAS good was that Kitty was getting into it. When she got bored with filming them going through boxes and writing things down, she decided to draw pictures of the babies from their photos, and have them grow up and put them in the situations Sophie and Fiona were describing in their stories.

"You are an excellent artist, Madam Munford," Artifacta told her one day before school when they sitting on the stage in the cafeteria behind the curtain, looking through their purple notebook for the thousandth time.

"I am?" Kitty said.

"I suggest that we follow these drawings and our pictures and our stories—"

"Based on our historical findings, of course," Sophie put in.

"Oh, yes—and I suggest we put them all into film form."

"Like a real movie?" Kitty said. Her big blue eyes were the size of dinner plates. Excited dinner plates, if that was possible.

Sophie, however, didn't jump up and hug the idea right away. She drew a circle over and over in the dust on the floor with her finger. "I think we need to do some more digging," she said. "Dr. Demetria Diggerty has more work to do."

The early bell rang, and Kitty scrambled for her backpack. When she was gone, Fiona leaned close to Sophie.

"I know what you're doing," she said.

"What?" Sophie said.

"You want to dig in your attic some more because you're obsessed with being adopted."

"What does obsessed mean?"

"It means you can't think about hardly anything else! And it's lame, Soph! Just because there aren't any pictures of you when you were a baby doesn't mean your parents aren't your birth parents!"

Sophie squinted at her, through her glasses, through the dimness. "If it were you," she said, "wouldn't you want to know for sure?"

"I think there are some things you just don't have to know," Fiona said.

Sophie couldn't settle in with that idea, even though it had come from Fiona, who knew almost everything. She was glad it was a Dr. Peter day, so she could at least talk to him about it.

But when Mama came to pick her up that afternoon, she said Mama and Daddy were having a session with Dr. Peter instead.

"You get to go home and relax," she said. "I made snowman cookies today, so you can have all you want. I think it's about time we got into the Christmas spirit around our house. Boppa's watching Zeke over at their house, so you have time to yourself for a while. Just keep the doors locked. You have my cell phone number—"

Mama was rattling on as if she couldn't get control of her tongue. Sophie didn't hear half of it. Once she got over being disappointed that she wasn't going to see Dr. Peter, she couldn't wait to get into the attic by herself and see if she could discover something new.

But it was what she didn't find that made the attic seem darker and darker. There was a box covered in what looked like a baby quilt, pushed back into the corner. Sophie knew they hadn't looked in this one, and her heart pounded as she opened it.

But inside were only two baby books—with things written in them about first teeth and first words and first birthday cakes. One was about Lacie. The other one was about Zeke.

Sophie was about to close the lid on them when she noticed that there were a bunch of pictures scattered in the bottom of the box. She scooped them out and leaned with them against Grandma Too's trunk with her flashlight.

They were all of a little girl, from about two years old until maybe five. She was a tiny thing, with skinny wrists and legs and hardly any hair, but Sophie could tell she wasn't a BABY baby because she was standing up and looking at books and hauling a huge stuffed rabbit that was even bigger than she was.

"That's Harold!" Sophie said out loud.

It was the bunny Mama's father had sent her one Christmas, and she'd had it until they moved from Houston and Mama said she was sure it would fall apart if they tried to pack it. Mama had told her that Sophie had insisted on naming him Harold, after Grandpa, because she'd heard Daddy say when she pulled him out of the wrappings that Christmas, "Why did Harold send her that? It's bigger than she is!"

Sophie shone the flashlight on the photo of her dragging Harold up a flight of stairs.

Then that must be me, she thought. *They did take pictures of me!*

That gave her a sudden burst of energy, and she plowed through the rest of the attic, searching for other boxes they might have missed. But there was nothing.

Sophie sat against the trunk again with the Harold snapshot in her hand. *It's like I didn't even exist until I was two years old,* she thought.

Maybe to them, I didn't.

Eight

Sophie didn't go up to her room as usual after supper that night, but instead she hung around with the rest of the family, and she studied them each carefully for signs.

She watched Zeke while he was tucked into the big chair in the family room with Daddy, together looking at the sports page.

Like Me: small for his age (but, then, so is Mama); brown eyes, only darker than mine; cute little turned up nose (but a lot of people have that).

Not Like Me: dark, thick, coarse hair that sticks up in all directions—like Daddy; half a smile, like Mama; a dimple in each side of his chin, like nobody; and very expressive eyebrows.

Sophie had never noticed that he even listened with his eyebrows. He was such a cute little brother, it made her want to cry.

She also surveyed Daddy as he told Zeke what teams were probably going to be in the Super Bowl.

Like Me: nothing.

Not Like Me: everything.

She moved on quickly to Mama, who was spread out on the couch writing out Christmas cards.

Like Me: light brown hair (like about half the people in the world); brown eyes (like about MOST of the people in the world); petite (because she exercises and she eats like a canary—hello!); high-pitched voice (who wouldn't with three kids?).

Not Like Me: pretty; nice; gets along with Daddy.

It wasn't looking good by the time she went upstairs to observe Lacie. It didn't help that the minute she stuck her head in the door, Lacie said, "If you're going to sit here and look at me like you're doing to everybody else, forget it. You're freaking me out."

Sophie switched to Plan B. "No—I wanted to ask you a question."

Lacie got her eyes about halfway rolled, and then she seemed to catch herself. She got up from her desk and flopped down on her bed and patted her mattress.

"Okay," she said. "Have a seat. I'll tell you anything you want to know."

Sophie could almost hear Daddy telling Lacie she wanted her to be a "role model" for Sophie. She resisted the urge to run out of there with what little of herself she had left, and instead sat on the corner of Lacie's bed.

"I'm not going to bite you," Lacie said. "Here—get comfortable."

She tossed Sophie a pillow shaped like a big fuzzy basketball. Sophie held it in front of her and looked around. It had been a while since she'd been in here. It was hard to "get comfortable" in a room where the walls were covered in huge pictures of women shooting baskets, women making soccer goals, women hitting homeruns. She was a little surprised to see a poster with the Ten Commandments on it tacked to the ceiling over the bed.

"What did you want to ask me?" Lacie said.

"I want to know if you remember when I was first born."

Lacie gave her a blank look. "How would I remember that? I was only two."

"I remember stuff from being two," Sophie said. "I remember getting Harold."

"You remember stories about getting Harold, but you couldn't possibly remember it yourself. I don't even remember you getting Harold, and I was four."

That's probably because you never pay attention to anything I'm doing anyway, Sophie thought.

"So what's the first thing you DO remember about me?" she said.

Lacie didn't linger on it for too long before she shrugged. "I don't know. You've just always been my little sister, as far back as I can remember, which is like when I was five — so you were three."

"You don't remember me being a baby?"

"Unh-uh. I remember Zeke as a baby. He was so precious. He was the first baby I ever got to hold."

"Oh," Sophie said.

"So — is that all you wanted to talk about?" Lacie said. "You don't want to know anything about middle school or boys or anything?"

"Uh, no," Sophie said. "That's all I wanted to know."

She got up and headed for the door.

"You can talk to me anytime," Lacie said. "When you're like this, I can actually have a conversation with you."

"When I'm like what?" Sophie said.

"Like — real."

"Oh," Sophie said again.

As she trudged next door to her own room, she thought, *If this is what being real feels like — it's not what I want to be.*

Sophie had a hard time staying out of No-God Land the next day. It was a heavy, dreary place, but it seemed to hold her within its walls. When at lunch she couldn't even get interested in the Corn Flakes' "Treasures," as they had decided to call the purple notebook, Fiona slapped it shut and said, "We're going to the bathroom."

Sophie followed her there, feeling the stares of the Wheaties behind her. They still sat with the Corn Flakes everyday at lunch, but ever since the day Maggie had brought up the psychiatrist thing, it was as if they were just there to observe, like they were window shopping.

In the restroom, Fiona shoved Sophie into a stall and closed the door behind them. Sophie had to sit down on the toilet seat to make room for both of them.

"Okay, you have to stop obsessing," Fiona said.

"I can't," Sophie said. "Not until I know for sure."

"Have you thought about just asking them?"

Sophie shook her head miserably. "They'd probably just lie to me. They've been doing it for nine years."

"Nine?"

"I was adopted when I was two, I think. That's when the pictures start."

"Okay—I am so over this," Fiona said. "I know a way that we can prove that you are NOT adopted."

"How?" Sophie said.

"I saw it on *Law and Order*. It's something about blood types and stuff."

"Blood?"

"We ask Mrs. Utley. If she doesn't know, then she shouldn't be teaching science, is what I say."

Sophie felt herself go as cold as the porcelain potty she was perched on.

"What's the matter?" Fiona said.

"Maybe you're right," Sophie said. "Maybe there are some things we don't really need to know."

"No way—because you aren't going to be okay until you find out. We're going to Mrs. Utley."

When they were finally in science class at the end of the day, Fiona waited until the students were all at work on the solar system assignment, and then she dragged Sophie up to Mrs. Utley's desk.

She grinned at them, all of her chins wiggling happily. "What are you two up to now?" she said.

"Serious question," Fiona said. "How can you use your blood to prove somebody is or isn't your parent?"

Mrs. Utley's chins all stopped moving. "That IS a serious question," she said. She looked closely at both of them before she went on.

"Well," Mrs. Utley said. "A person would have to have his or her own DNA compared to the DNA of the parent in question. You understand that, right?"

"Is it expensive to do that?" Fiona said.

Fiona! Sophie wanted to say. *How am I going to get blood from Daddy?*

"Very," Mrs. Utley said. "Now, blood type, which just about everybody knows about themselves, can't tell you that someone IS your parent, but it CAN tell you if someone ISN'T. There are some blood types that could not possibly come from the combination of two other people's blood types."

"Do you know how to figure that out?" Fiona said.

"Yes," Mrs. Utley said. She was still watching them closely. The chins were very still. "One thing that is very basic is that if, say, you have the same blood type as your mother or your father, then it's possible that the one with that blood type is your parent—but it doesn't prove it. Beyond that, I would have to know the exact blood types involved." She folded her plump hands on her desk. "Now, do you want to tell me why we're having this conversation?"

"Research," Fiona said. "Thanks."

The minute Sophie brought up blood types at the dinner table that night, Daddy broke into a grin.

"At last—some interest in science! Some project for school, huh?"

Sophie didn't have time to deny it. Daddy was already going around the table, pointing.

"Your mother is A positive. Zeke is A positive. Lacie is A negative—"

"I've always been special," Lacie said, flashing a cheesy smile.

"And you, Soph, are AB positive. I know that for sure, because it's the same as mine."

"And a good thing too," Mama said.

"Why?" Lacie said.

"What's for dessert?" Daddy said.

"I'm not done yet!" Zeke wailed.

Sophie let them argue that out in a blur beyond her as she sorted things through. So Daddy COULD be her father. But Mrs. Utley had said that didn't mean he definitely WAS her father. She was really no closer to knowing than she had been before.

Later she padded downstairs to have Daddy check over her math homework. She got almost to the bottom step, when she heard Mama talking to him. They were sitting at the snack bar, having their decaf and, obviously, a serious conversation. All Sophie heard was Mama saying, "Rusty, I just think it's time she knew."

That was all Sophie had to hear. She crept back up the stairs, clutching her math homework in her sweaty hand.

Sophie didn't even have a chance to tell Fiona and Kitty the next morning before Maggie was suddenly there in the hallway with them.

"I know you said you didn't want to know," she said, without a hi or anything, "but I think you should let me tell you about the rumor that's being spread about you."

Sophie was sure she couldn't carry another thing in her mind. ALL the space, God or No-God, was being taken up with the biggest worry on the planet.

"Why does she need to know it?" Fiona said.

"Because it's getting worse," Maggie said. "And it's going to keep getting worse if Sophie doesn't stop it."

"The only reason it's getting worse for me is because YOU keep bringing it up!" someone shouted, someone who didn't sound like Sophie, but was. "I told you, I DON'T WANT TO KNOW. So leave me alone! Just leave me alone!"

Everyone in the hallway outside the Language Arts room stopped and stared. Even Fiona's jaw had dropped. Kitty was whimpering.

But it was Maggie who looked the most stunned of all. She took a step backward and let the cement look take over her eyes, but not before Sophie saw the flash of hurt go through them.

"I'm sorry," Sophie said. Her voice was already shaking.

"Too bad," Maggie said. "Now you're just gonna have to find out for yourself."

She stomped into the room, passing Mr. Denton on the way.

"Everything all right out here?" he said.

"No," somebody said. "Sophie just pitched a fit, right in Maggie's face."

It was Anne-Stuart reporting. Fiona groaned under her breath.

"As if she gives a rip about Maggie," she whispered.

"Thanks for the update, Anne-Stuart," Mr. Denton said.

He smiled at her until she gave up and went on into the room, followed by B.J. and Willoughby, who looked as if they were about to belch.

"You okay, Sophie?" Mr. Denton said when they were gone.

"Yes, sir," Sophie lied.

The bell rang.

"Take a minute and then come on in," he said, and he closed the classroom door.

Fiona and Sophie were left in the hall.

"You go, girl," Fiona said.

"What?"

"Way to stand up to Maggie. She was pushing way too hard."

"I shouldn't have yelled at her like that."

"Like you had a choice! If you hadn't, she would have kept standing there poking at you until you listened to her stupid rumor. You don't need that, and I was proud of you."

But as Sophie trailed behind her into the classroom, she felt anything but proud. There was no place for feeling good about yourself in the Land of No God.

One thing was sure, though, she decided as the day dragged on with people—especially the Corn Pops—staring at her and whispering behind their hands. She had to ask Mama or Daddy for the truth.

And it certainly wasn't hard to decide which one to go to. Mama might stand behind Daddy on everything he said, but at least she didn't yell.

Sophie worked up to it all day, ignoring the whispers and stares at lunch and during classes and trying to imagine herself talking to Mama. It seemed odd to her that even though she didn't TRY to picture Jesus as she planned her approach, his kind face kept popping up, when she least expected it.

Okay, okay, she told him. *I'll obey whatever they tell me. But I still think I have a right to know.*

She was completely ready when she got off the bus and walked "sedately" as Fiona would put it, up to the back door. The question for Mama was already on her lips when she stepped into the kitchen and found Boppa at the sink.

"Hello, little wisp of a girl," Boppa said to her. He was smiling his usual I'm-happy-to-see-you smile, but the eyes beneath the caterpillar eyebrows were sad.

"Where's Mama?" she said.

Boppa put a glass of milk on the snack bar and motioned for her to sit.

"Where is she?" Sophie said. "There's something wrong, I know it."

"There is," Boppa said. "Your mama went to Minneapolis. Her dad—your grandpa—is very sick. She's gone to see him."

"Is she coming back?" Sophie said.

"Of course she's coming back," Boppa said. "But she's your grandpa's only kid, and since there isn't a grandma anymore, it's up to your mama to take care of him."

Sophie looked hopefully into Boppa's eyes. "So am I coming to stay at your house?"

"You know, I'd really like that," Boppa said. "But you kids are going to stay here with your dad. Your mama wants the family together."

"Oh," Sophie said.

And she felt the No-God space grow bigger.

Nine

Lacie was the next one to come home and find out about Mama. To Sophie's utter AMAZEMENT, she immediately burst into tears.

"Mama can't be gone!" she cried. "I NEED her!"

"Your dad will be home shortly," Boppa said. He looked as if he wished Daddy would walk in the door within the next seven seconds.

"I don't want him! He won't understand!"

Sophie shifted from "amazed" to "absolutely flabbergasted."

Lacie dumped her backpack on the floor and flung both hands up to her face. "I failed my English quiz!"

"You?" Sophie said.

"I read the wrong story! And if I get below a C on my progress report, Coach won't let me play in the next game—and I'm the CAPTAIN!"

"Lacie, I think your father will understand," Boppa said.

"No!" Lacie said. "He'll yell! He'll say I wasn't responsible—"

"Not aware of your surroundings," Sophie said.

"I KNOW! Shut UP!"

Lacie slid down the wall and sat on the floor and sobbed. That woke Zeke up from his nap, and the minute he saw Lacie crying, he started. Sophie was about to escape to the attic in search of Dr. Demetria Diggerty when Daddy walked in with a bag with Chinese writing on it.

He took one look at the two crumpled heaps on the floor, said good-bye to Boppa, and made the three of them sit up at the snack bar, containers in front of them, chopsticks in hand. He stood across from them, leaning on the stove, and said,

"Okay, one at a time. Zeke—you first—you're the loudest." Daddy looked at Lacie. "You think you can hold it in for five minutes?"

Lacie gave a miserable nod.

"What's up, Z?"

"I want Mama!"

"I do too, pal," Daddy said. "The good news is, she'll be back. The even better news is, this means a lot of McDonald's."

"Every day?" Zeke said.

"Whatever it takes," Daddy said.

Zeke tore into his fortune cookies, and Daddy turned to Lacie.

"Next. What's with the tears?"

Lacie poured out her story, crying all over her chow mein. Although Sophie saw Daddy's face-muscles twitch, he just said, "No problem. I'll talk to your teacher—we'll get it straightened out."

"But when? You'll be at work all day!"

"I'm working at home in the afternoon while your mom's gone. I'll pick Zeke up from kindergarten and be here when you girls get home from school." He straightened up from the stove. "I'm Mama until the real Mama gets back."

Sophie put her chopsticks down. Fried rice suddenly tasted like sawdust.

Sure—you're going to go stand up for Lacie with her teacher, even though her mistake was HER OWN FAULT! she felt like yelling at him. *But you haven't even ASKED me if I have any problems.*

But Sophie decided right then he couldn't help her anyway. He wasn't enough Mama for that.

Which was why the next morning she practically RAN straight from the bus to Mr. Denton's room without looking for Fiona and Kitty. She didn't want Fiona grilling her about whether she had asked about the adoption.

Mr. Denton was grading papers when she arrived, and she tried to skip past him to go back to her locker. There was really nobody she wanted to have a conversation with. But he looked up and smiled at her.

"Sophie!" he said. "Just the person I need to talk to."

Sophie dragged herself back to his desk. "I want to recommend you for the Gifted and Talented Program," he said. "You know, GATE. I need for you to take this letter and application home and have your mom or dad help you fill it out, and then one of them needs to sign it."

Sophie stared at the papers he held out to her.

"Me?" she said.

"Of course, you," Mr. Denton said. "And Fiona. And Kitty."

"Why?" Sophie said.

Mr. Denton leaned back in his chair with his eyebrows scrambled together. "Because you're three of the most creative students I've ever had. You all need to be in GATE." His lips twitched. "Unless you don't WANT to, of course—"

"I do!" Sophie said. "Thank you!"

Suddenly, she could feel her chest going loose, as if some space were opening up in there. Maybe God was coming back ...

When Fiona arrived she slipped into the table beside Sophie and went straight to a piece of news.

"The Corn Pops are passing a notebook around to each other," she whispered "They're writing in it."

"What do you think it means?" Sophie said.

"I think it means they're trying to be like US. Theirs isn't purple, of course."

"Of course," Sophie said.

She had an open and light and good feeling, and she couldn't wait to get home that afternoon and show Daddy the application. Maybe it didn't even matter if he was her birth parent or not, as long as he was proud of her.

He was at the dining room table with his laptop computer and his cell phone and his electronic organizer. Zeke was at the other end of the table, chowing down on a Happy Meal.

Sophie just put the application in front of Daddy and waited for his face to beam.

But it didn't.

He studied the form and the letter for a long time. With each minute that passed, Sophie could feel her open space closing up again. Finally, she couldn't stand it.

"Aren't you proud of me?" she said.

"I'm happy your teacher thinks this much of you," he said. "And he's right—you're definitely creative."

There was such a huge "but" in his voice, Sophie could almost see it.

"But, Soph," he said, "I'm not sure you're ready for this. I'm not convinced you have the basics down yet."

Sophie stared at him. Her chest was closing in like something was pressing against it.

"You mean, you're not gonna let me do it?" she said.

"I mean I need to think about it," he said.

You just DO that! Sophie wanted to shout at him. *I should have known you would find a reason not to believe in me. You would sure let Lacie do it!*

It occurred to her as she stormed up the stairs to the attic that as far as she knew, Lacie had never even been asked to be in GATE. But that didn't help.

Dr. Demetria Diggerty rested against the closed door of the excavation site and closed her eyes. Master LaCroix was more evil than she had imagined. How was she to fight him? How was she to rise to the top of her career with him forever holding her back?

And then the famous archaeologist opened her eyes, and she lifted her chin. How? How indeed! By refusing to give up. Yes, she must obey him as long as he WAS her master. But what if he wasn't?

Tearing off her coat and rolling up her sleeves, Dr. Diggerty headed straight for the boxes that had not yet been unearthed. There must be some important paper that would tell her what she needed to know.

The sun lowered and slowly turned the site dim, but Dr. Demetria Diggerty dug on, through box after box, poring over papers written in some ancient language too difficult to understand. It was only when in desperation she opened the last box that she found what she was looking for. The moment she read its first line, the document fell from her fingers to the floor —

Sophie stood staring at it. She could hardly see it anymore through the blur of her tears. But she knew she would never forget the only line she had read—the only line she needed to read:

Thank you for your interest in adopting a child.

Sophie couldn't do her homework that night. She wouldn't talk to Fiona on the phone. She told Lacie she felt sick and shouldn't eat dinner.

"She really misses Mama," she heard Lacie tell Daddy. "I think we should just leave her alone."

They did—although Sophie knew she could have been surrounded by a thousand people and she still would have felt alone. She was deep into No-God space, and there was no room there for anyone else.

She got herself up and dressed early the next morning and went out to the bus stop long before it was time to, so she didn't have to say much to Daddy. She tried to imagine what Dr. Diggerty would do, but she realized right away that she didn't want to go there. It was Dr. Diggerty who had revealed all this in the first place. If it wasn't for all the digging into the past, maybe Sophie would never have discovered this thing about her life.

And imagining Jesus? That was out of the question. The minute she brought him to mind, she shut him out. She was mad at him. She was mad at God.

She was pretty much mad at everybody.

The bus was at least warm, and when she got on board, she hurried, head down, to her usual seat. As always, Harley and Gill were sitting in front of her, but they didn't turn around. They seemed to be busy with a green binder that they were both reading from. That was okay with Sophie. She didn't want to talk anyway.

Not even Fiona could console her during the day. Sophie couldn't even tell her what she had found. The words just wouldn't come out of her mouth.

She was headed for the bus that afternoon when Daddy was suddenly there beside her. Sophie froze right inside her jacket.

"I can ride the bus," she said.

"I'm taking you to see Dr. Peter," he said.

"It's not my day!"

"It is now," Daddy said.

He wasn't yelling and his face wasn't red and his jaws weren't twitching as he talked about nothing all the way to

Hampton. But he didn't ask her why she was sitting there chewing at her gloves and banging her feet against the front of the seat, either. He didn't even tell her why she was going to Dr. Peter's.

And Sophie didn't ask.

It was even hard to talk to Dr. Peter. She wrapped her arms around one of the face pillows and squeezed it and forced herself not to tell him she had found out she was adopted.

What if he already knows? she thought.

Sophie squeezed the pillow hard. That would mean that her Dr. Peter was now lying to her too, by keeping it from her. That might be the worse thought of all.

"So," Dr. Peter said finally. "Must be tough with just your dad at home. He says you're having a hard time."

Sophie nodded, but she clamped her teeth together so she wouldn't be tempted to blurt out something.

"Wow," he said. "I can feel that anger all the way over here."

She glared at him.

"You mad at your father?"

"Yes," Sophie said, teeth still clenched. "And I'm mad at God too, so I don't even want to talk about him."

Dr. Peter picked up a face pillow, the one with the wart on the end of its nose. "She's so mad at God, she isn't even speaking to him."

Sophie chewed at her lip and banged her feet against the front of the window seat.

"That's what it's like when you love somebody," Dr. Peter said to the pillow. "You can get so mad at 'em, you can't even talk to them."

"I don't love Daddy right now!" Sophie said.

She chomped down with her teeth again, but not so hard this time. Maybe it would be okay to tell Dr. Peter SOME of

216

it. "I got recommended for GATE," she said, "only HE won't sign the permission paper because he says I'm not ready. He doesn't even know anything about me!"

"Ouch," Dr. Peter said. "That does hurt."

"I know," Sophie said, "and I don't want to talk about it."

"That's fine," Dr. Peter said. "Then why don't I talk for a minute?"

Sophie slouched back against the pillows and watched him form his words in his eyes.

"You say you're mad at Jesus right now, so let me tell you about somebody else. You remember John the Baptist, the one who baptized Jesus?"

"His cousin," Sophie said, before she clamped her mouth shut again.

"Right. John gathered friends around him, friends like you have, and, just like you, he picked them very carefully." The eyes sparkled. "Not just any old person can be a Corn Flake, right? You have to have imagination and not be all about yourself and be willing to take risks."

Sophie just nodded.

"Now, I want you to try to imagine yourself sitting down with John as one of his Corn Flakes. And I want you to think of him saying these words to you. You ready?"

"Sure," Sophie said. It couldn't hurt, even if it didn't help.

"John's friends were asking him if he was upset because suddenly a bunch of people were going to Jesus to be baptized, instead of to him. They wanted to know what was up with that. John was their main man!" Dr. Peter rubbed his palms together. "John told them Jesus was God's Son—the Real Deal—and whoever accepted and trusted the Son got in on everything—a complete life here and a forever life after they left the earth."

Sophie didn't see how this applied to her.

"But—" Dr. Peter said, holding up a finger, "he also told them that the person who avoids and distrusts the Son is in the dark and doesn't see life. To that person, God is just an angry darkness."

Dr. Peter gave Sophie a smile that reminded her of the kind eyes she'd seen in her mind so many times. She fought back the tears that were making her throat tight.

"You've already learned that God loves you, Loodle," he said. "Now that you know that, it's your job to love him, always, with all your heart, no matter what happens. It's okay to be angry with him, but you can't stop loving him. If you do, all you have is angry darkness."

"No-God space," Sophie said.

Dr. Peter nodded and sat back. Sophie pulled some hair into a moustache under her nose and blinked her eyes hard so she wouldn't cry those tears. Dr. Peter tilted his head at her.

"I haven't seen you do that in a long time, Loodle," he said. "And I think we need to do something about it."

"Like what?" Sophie said.

"Like talk to Jesus, first of all, no matter how mad you are at him. AND talk to your dad, no matter how angry you are with HIM. He needs to at least know how important this GATE program is to you." He wrinkled his glasses up his nose as he watched her. "I would be willing to bet that you didn't try very hard to discuss this with him."

"No," Sophie said. "I went to the attic and turned into Dr. Diggerty."

Dr. Peter grinned. "I love that honesty, Loodle. Okay, so if you can, be that honest with your father too. Tell him how you feel." He looked at the face pillow again. "What has she got to lose?" he said.

Ten

Sophie thought about that for halfway home in the car with Daddy before she decided Dr. Peter was right. She didn't have anything else to lose.

She wriggled sideways in her seat belt and said, "I really want to be in the GATE program, and I know I can do it because I'm making all A's and B's now and I never ever did that before in my whole life."

She hated it that her voice was high-pitched and shaky, so she stopped. She straightened back around and stared at gray Hampton as it turned into Poquoson. There. She had been honest.

"Then here's the game plan," Daddy said. "I'll let you go into GATE, but if your grades drop even a half a point in any subject, I'm pulling you out. Can you deal with that?"

Sophie could only stare at him and nod. The minute she got home, she took the form and a pen to him, before he could change his mind.

But she still didn't feel open and light and good again, even when she put the signed application on Mr. Denton's desk the next morning. When she went back out into the hall to go look for Fiona and Kitty, Anne-Stuart suddenly emerged from the little knot of Corn Pops as Sophie passed and fell into step beside her.

"So you turned in your application," she said.

"How did you know?" Sophie said.

"We saw you come in with it."

Sophie stopped so she could look straight at the sniffly Anne-Stuart. "Are all of y'all in it?" she said.

"Just me and Julia—we got in last year, so we automatically get to apply again."

"Oh," Sophie said.

She tried to move on, but Anne-Stuart grabbed her sleeve.

"I just don't want you to get your hopes up," Anne-Stuart said. "Just because Mr. Denton picks you, doesn't mean you'll get in. OTHER people look at you for OTHER things."

"What 'other things'?" Sophie said.

"Well," Anne-Stuart said, slowly, as if she DIDN'T already know EXACTLY what she was going to say. "They want to find out if you have a lot of problems. Not like with school-work, but OTHER problems." She let go of Sophie's sleeve and gave her shoulder a pat. "I just thought you should know that before you got too excited about getting in."

Sophie refused to watch Anne-Stuart as she returned to the waiting Corn Pops. She held her own head high until she was around the corner and had passed through the double doors into the hall that led to the cafeteria. As soon as she knew she was out of sight, she let her shoulders drop, and she made her way somehow behind the curtains on the stage, where she sank to the floor.

She's right, Sophie thought. *I do have problems.*

And Dr. Peter, it seemed, was wrong—because she didn't even want to try to find the God-space right now.

Once again, Fiona, and even Kitty, tried to cheer her up during the day. When science class was over and Sophie was headed out for the bus, Fiona pressed the purple notebook into her hands.

"At least take this home, Demetria," she said. "It will fill the hours."

"I'm not Demetria," Sophie said. "I don't know WHO I am."

But Fiona's gray eyes drooped so suddenly and so far down, Sophie took the "Treasures." She didn't look at it on the bus, though, even when every other girl on there gathered around that same green binder she'd seen Gill and Harley with, reading as if it contained all the secrets of the universe. Nobody invited her to look at it with them, not even the Wheaties, but that was okay. She didn't care.

Daddy made her eat McDonald's with them before she escaped to her room that night. It seemed to her to be cruel and unusual punishment, as Fiona would have said, to have to consume rubber French fries while listening to Lacie gush to Daddy about how wonderful he had been with her English teacher.

"She's letting me retake the quiz!" she said.

"Score," Daddy said. And they high-fived each other.

"May I be excused?" Sophie said.

The minute she was in her room, however, she realized that she'd left her backpack downstairs.

I'm gonna wait until everybody's off doing their thing before I go down and get it, she decided. *I can't listen to Lacie anymore.*

But as she sprawled across her bed, it was hard for Sophie NOT to hear Lacie in her head — because she wanted so much to be saying things like that herself.

Daddy — thank you SO much for standing up for me!

Daddy — you are my hero.

Daddy — you're the best. I mean, the BEST.

Sophie closed her eyes to try to shut it out. Jesus was there, before she even tried to imagine him.

He didn't say anything—of course. Dr. Peter had told her many times that she could only imagine Jesus and talk to him and then wait for him to answer in one of the many ways he did his work.

But his eyes were different this time. They were still kind, but they were also stern—and not like Daddy-stern, just please-listen-to-me firm, the way Dr. Peter's had been that very day.

"Okay," Sophie whispered. "I'll listen."

It was strangely quiet. Even Zeke wasn't banging on something or wailing for Mama. But Sophie didn't hear anything.

I should listen to the Bible, she thought. That was the OTHER thing Dr. Peter kept telling her. Just that day—what was that thing about darkness? Angry darkness . . .

Suddenly, Sophie began to shiver. "I don't want to be in the dark anymore," she whispered. "It's scary here."

She could feel something wet trailing into each ear. "I'm sorry I thought I didn't love you," she whispered. *But I'm so mad—*

Sophie lay there for a long time after that. It got dark in her room. But it wasn't quite so dark inside her.

After a while, there was a knock on the door, and Lacie stuck her head in and snapped on the light.

"Are you okay?" she said.

"Yes," Sophie said. She sat up, squinting, and turned away so Lacie wouldn't see the tears.

"I miss her too," Lacie said.

Sophie started to face her, wanted to say, "Isn't it heinous, Lacie?" But Lacie was already halfway out the door.

"Daddy wanted me to make sure you were doing your homework," she said.

When Lacie was gone, Sophie hauled herself off the bed and scrubbed the tears away with her fists before she put her glasses back on.

I'm going to obey and I'm going to love, she told herself firmly as she went down the steps. *No matter how mad I get.*

When she got to the family room, Daddy was sitting in his chair, thumbing through a book.

It was "Treasures."

That's my private property! she wanted to scream at him. *It's none of your business!*

She reached down, snatched up her open backpack from the floor, and tore back up the stairs. Whether Daddy saw or heard her or not, she didn't know. The next morning, she stalked to the bus stop without the purple notebook.

You're REALLY going to have to help me, Jesus, she prayed. *Because this is MEGA-hard.*

She got to school ahead of Fiona again, and she went straight to her locker. The minute she got there, she knew something was wrong. The door was already partway open.

Sophie pulled it open the rest of the way, and something fell out on her feet.

It was a green binder.

I'm not touching that, Sophie thought. *I know they put it in here so they could say I stole it or something.*

Sophie was tempted to leave it there on the floor, until she saw a bright pink Post-It Note sticking out of the pages. Someone had printed in tidy letters: SOPHIE READ THIS!

Sophie picked up the binder and stuffed it into her backpack. Without even saying hi to Mr. Denton, she hurried to the cafeteria stage, parked near a narrow opening in the curtain so she could see to read, and opened the binder.

She scanned the other pages first, and as she read, she could feel her eyes bulging.

There was a page for every girl in sixth grade, even in the other classes. The name was written at the top, and below it, each one in a different colored gel pan, other people had written comments about them. No one had signed any of the comments, but it didn't take a rocket scientist to figure out who had written most of them. Not only was there a bra size written at the top of each page, but most of the comments—except for those about the Corn Pops—were harsh and ugly and heinous.

They said Fiona thought she was all that because she had a lot of money.

They said Kitty was a whiner and a baby and was never loyal to anybody.

They said Vette and Nikki were really boys because all they talked about was cars, and no real girl would do that.

Julia got comments like she is the prettiest girl in the whole school—and the nicest.

Anne-Stuart was rewarded with—*totally smart. Smarter than Fiona even THINKS she is.*

B.J.—*a friend you can totally count on.*

By the time she had skimmed through the binder, Sophie was terrified to turn to the page marked, SOPHIE READ THIS! But there seemed to be a strange pull on her fingers as she turned to the pink Post-It Note. There was no way she couldn't read it.

The first comment was written in ice-blue ink. *Soapie LaCroix is so weerd. We all know she's way behind diveloping— she has NO breasts at all and probly never will. But she's behind-in-the-mind too.*

In turquoise ink, someone else had picked up the theme. *She has to see a shrink because she's a syko—psycko—crazy.*

The person with the green pen had written: *I used to think it was totally strange that she could be such a freek and her sister Lacey at the middle school could be so totally kewl. But now it makes total sense. She's adopted, and she's too stoopid to know it.*

Sophie was shaking so hard she had to grip the edges of the binder to hold onto it.

But it was the final comment on the page that finally brought her to big, choking sobs. The last girl had written in red: *The only reason her parents adopted her was because they felt sorry for her and they probably didn't even really want her. Who DOES?*

Not the GATE program, said the one with the blue pen. She had taken another turn so she could write: *We really need to make sure Mr. Denton and the GATE people know about all this. We DO NOT want her in our program!!!!!!!!!!!!!!!!!!!!!!!!!!!*

When Fiona and Kitty found Sophie on the stage, she was crying so hard she couldn't talk. She just handed the binder to Fiona and kept sobbing.

It didn't take long for Fiona to read the Sophie page, with Kitty gasping beside her, and to hurl the whole binder across the stage. It landed with a dusty splash in the corner.

"That is where that trash BELONGS!" Fiona said. Even in the back-stage dimness, Sophie could see her gray eyes blazing as she paced. "All right, I have HAD IT with all of this heinous behavior. First of all, none of that is true, Sophie LaCroix, and I don't want you believing a word of it."

"But I AM flat-chested," Sophie said. "And I DO see a therapist. And I AM adopted."

Fiona stopped pacing. "You know that for sure?"

"I found a paper about it."

"Did you ask your dad about it?"

"I'm waiting for Mama to come home. But I already have the proof."

Kitty sank to the floor beside Sophie and hugged her. Fiona went back to walking back and forth, each step startling up sneezy clouds.

"Okay, so maybe you're adopted," she said, "but no one could know why. They're just making stuff up to be their usual heinous selves."

"How did they even know THIS much stuff?" Kitty said, pointing to the offensive binder in the corner.

"They spy, I know they do," Fiona said. "In the bathroom—in the classroom—they're always around." She stopped, hands on hips. "That isn't the point. The point is, they have to PAY."

Kitty looked up at her, eyes fearful. "What do you mean 'pay'?"

"No," Sophie said. She pulled her face away from Kitty's shoulder. "The point is, the next thing they're going to do is accuse me of stealing their binder."

"But you didn't," Kitty said.

"Of course she didn't," Fiona said. "But since when did the truth make any difference to them?"

"So put it back in one of THEIR lockers," Kitty said.

Sophie shook her head. "I don't know any of their combinations."

"But somebody knew yours."

Kitty and Sophie both looked at Fiona. She was standing perfectly still, eyes aglow.

"Nobody knows my combination but you guys," Sophie said. "I never give it out to anybody that isn't a Corn Flake."

Fiona knelt down beside them and lowered her voice to its best revelation-level.

"Then anybody who has ever BEEN a Corn Flake would still have it," she said. "Now, wouldn't she?"

Three heads slowly nodded. And three Corn Flake mouths said, "Maggie."

Eleven

Before the last bell rang, the Corn Flakes had a plan.

The first step was to confront Maggie. It wasn't hard to find her, because she was always sitting properly in her seat when the bell rang, sharpened pencil at the ready and the assignment already copied off of the board.

When Mr. Denton said he wanted them to get into groups to work on their story questions, Fiona, Kitty, and Sophie had Maggie surrounded in seconds.

"How many times do I have to tell you?" Maggie said through tight lips. "I don't want—"

"This isn't about what you do or don't want," Fiona said. "It's about what you have to do."

Sophie could tell Kitty was holding back a whimper. That was her only assignment for this first step: not to start crying.

"You put that evil green binder in my locker, Maggie," Sophie said. "And you should help us get it back to where it belongs before the Corn Pops accuse me of stealing it."

"It belongs in the trash," Maggie said. "I was hoping you would throw it away after you read it."

Three pairs of Corn Flake eyes bulged at her.

"Then why did you make me read it at all?" Sophie said.

"Because you wouldn't listen to me, and I knew they were planning to keep you from getting into GATE."

"Was that the rumor you kept telling us was going around?" Fiona said. "All that stuff they said about Sophie in the book?"

"Why do you even care if I get into GATE or not?" Sophie said. "I thought you hated us."

"I don't hate anybody," Maggie said. Her face set into its usual hard mold. "I'm a good person."

Fiona leaned in, pulling the rest of them with her. "A good person would help us get that binder back to the Corn Pops before they say Sophie stole it." She glanced over her shoulder at the shiny-haired group giggling in the corner. "I'm surprised they haven't accused her already."

"They think I have it so I could write comments about you guys," Maggie said. "I asked them for it."

"Oh," Sophie said.

She glanced at Fiona, who actually looked impressed. "You have more imagination than I gave you credit for, Maggie," Fiona said.

That got a grunt from Maggie.

"Okay, then this is simple," Fiona said. "Since you asked them for it, you can just give it back to them."

"I think you oughta turn them in," Maggie said.

Kitty let go of a whimper.

Sophie shook her head. "Nobody signed their names on their comments," she said. "Even if we took it straight to the principal's office, we can't prove they did it."

"Good thinking, Demetria," Fiona said.

"I thought she was Antoinette," Maggie said.

"I think we should go on with our plan," Sophie said.

"Which is?" Maggie said. The words had stopped thudding.

"We get the binder back to them, and then we go to them as a whole group and we tell them what they're doing is wrong and that we WON'T tell if they promise to destroy it."

"What if that doesn't work?" Kitty said. Her voice was curling up into a whine. "You even said we can't prove they did it."

"I don't think they're smart enough to figure that out," Fiona said.

"I think we're in the right space if we do that." Sophie put out her pinky, and Fiona pinkied with it, and so did Kitty. "Maggie?" she said.

"You want me to do the handshake?" she said.

"It doesn't mean you have to be a Corn Flake," Sophie said. "It just means you're agreeing to the plan."

Maggie stuck out her finger like it was a club and hooked it around Sophie's. Then Sophie reached into her backpack and pulled out the green binder. She held it by a corner with two fingers as she passed it to Maggie. Kitty was holding her nose.

Just as Maggie was about to take it in her hands, two other hands reached down, and suddenly the binder was above their heads. Mr. Denton was holding it.

"Why don't I just remove this little distraction so you ladies can get back to work?" he said. "You can pick it up from me after school."

Sophie's heart stopped. Mr. Denton took the binder to his desk and tossed it on top of a pile of papers.

"It's okay—it's okay—" Fiona whispered. "They didn't see."

As Kitty wilted beside her, Sophie glanced back at the Corn Pops who were so into their giggle-fest they didn't seem aware that there was even a classroom around them.

"What if Mr. Denton reads it?" Sophie said.

"Maybe he should," Maggie said.

"But what if he thinks WE did it!" Kitty said.

"Yes, we would so write all those heinous things about ourselves," Fiona said.

"Ladies . . ."

Sophie flipped open her literature book and motioned for everybody else to do the same. Somehow they got through the assignment—and their next two classes—but Sophie knew that for her part it was only because she just kept thinking, *We're still in God-space.*

Maggie stuck to them like they were all sharing an oxygen mask. She even sat with them at lunch. The Wheaties didn't. They were at another table with their backs to the Corn Flakes.

"What did we ever do to them?" Kitty said.

"I bet the Corn Pops got to them," Fiona said. "But they'll figure it out."

"Speaking of Corn Pops," Maggie muttered.

Sophie looked up to see B.J. approaching. She was obviously on a mission, because her cheeks were the color of two red Christmas balls, and her eyes were narrowed down into slits. She stopped several feet from their table, as if she didn't want to catch something contagious, and slanted the slits at Maggie.

"We have to talk, Maggie," she said.

Maggie didn't even look at B.J. "I got nothing to say."

"Well, I have plenty to say, ladies."

They all jerked around to see Mr. Denton standing at the end of the table. His entire HEAD was red.

"And these are most of the people I want to say it to." He looked at B.J. "If you'll excuse us."

B.J. bolted back to the Corn Pops table, and Mr. Denton sat down next to Fiona, across from Sophie. The rest of the cafeteria went into a low hum.

Without saying another word, Mr. Denton reached inside his tweed blazer and pulled out the green binder. He let it fall to the table in front of him with a thump that went right into Sophie's chest and stayed there.

"It isn't ours, Mr. Denton," Fiona said. "We didn't make it."

"We didn't even write in it!" Kitty said. She was already crying.

"I don't want to think that you did," Mr. Denton said. "I don't want to think that anyone I know took part in this. It's the most appalling thing I've ever read."

"It's definitely heinous," Fiona said.

Mr. Denton nodded. "I can't think of a better word for it. If you didn't create this hideous piece of filth, then who did?"

"Julia, B.J., Anne-Stuart, and Willoughby."

They all looked at Maggie. Each name had thudded to the tabletop next to the binder.

"I know because I saw them doing it, and I got it from them so I could show it to Sophie."

Mr. Denton closed his eyes for a second. "You're telling me the truth?" he said. "No exaggeration? No stretching the facts?"

"That's SO not Maggie's style," Fiona said.

"Julia," Mr. Denton called out without even turning around. "Stop right there."

Sophie watched in amazement as Julia and the other Corn Pops froze halfway to the door. They couldn't have looked more guilty if they had been tiptoeing out of a bank in ski masks with bulging bags.

"Yes, sir?" Julia said.

Mr. Denton turned to look at them. "Over here," he said.

The faces of the Corn Pops behind Julia went white. But the instant Mr. Denton turned back around, Julia gave them

231

all a hard look and fixed a smile on her face. Three more heads came up, three more manes of hair were tossed, and four poster girls for Getting Away with Anything approached the table.

"Sit," Mr. Denton said.

Julia curled her lip. "Where?"

"Down," he said.

The Corn Flakes bunched together so the Corn Pops could gather at the end of the table. Willoughby tried to lean on Julia but she brushed her away. Anne-Stuart sniffed, and B.J. grabbed a napkin and thrust it at her. They all smiled at Mr. Denton in unison.

"What's up, Mr. D.?" Julia said.

Mr. Denton picked up the binder and let it drop again.

All four sets of Corn Pop eyes went to Maggie. She didn't even flinch.

"I understand you are responsible for this," Mr. Denton said.

"Us?" B.J. said. "Are our names on it or something?"

"No, but your handwriting is. I've graded enough of your papers to know it when I see it."

"We didn't—" Anne-Stuart started to say.

But Julia stopped her with the tiniest shake of thick hair. "We aren't the only ones, Mr. Denton," she said. "We would never have thought of doing a Slam Book if they hadn't started it first." She tossed the hair at Sophie and Fiona.

"I don't even know what a Slam Book is!" Kitty wailed.

"She's still such a whiner," Sophie heard Willoughby mutter to Anne-Stuart.

"What do you mean, 'they started it'?" Mr. Denton said. "You're saying there's another one of these floating around?"

"Yes," Julia said. She swept her eyes over the Corn Pops, who all nodded like a panel of judges. "It's purple and they treat it like it's the Bible or something."

"We saw them passing it around to each other," Anne-Stuart said, "and Willoughby said it was a Slam Book."

Willoughby looked a little stricken, until B.J. nudged her with an elbow.

"Didn't you tell your mom about it and she said it sounded like the Slam Books she and her friends used to keep when she was a kid?"

Willoughby gave a poodle-like yip, which Sophie assumed was a "yes."

"That explanation is supposed to clear this up for me?" Mr. Denton said. "You THOUGHT these girls had a Slam Book, so you felt like you needed to start one too?"

The Corn Pops looked at Julia. Sophie could almost see her fighting under her own skin to somehow come out still being the poster girl. It was almost sad.

"You know what?" Julia said. Her eyes suddenly sparkled with tears. "Ever since we got in trouble for the way we treated Kitty, everybody has been thinking that these girls —" She passed a hand over Fiona and Sophie's heads. "They think these girls are the greatest thing, like, ever — and we're the bad girls all of a sudden." She waved her fingers in front of her eyes, as if she were trying to dry up the tears that Sophie wasn't sure were really there to begin with. "We just thought that if we did what they were doing, everybody would think we were all wonderful too."

Sophie looked at Fiona. There was an OH PUH-LEEZE plastered all over her face.

"No, Julia," Mr. Denton said. "You thought if you could EXPOSE what they were doing, everybody would think they were worse than you are. Wasn't that really the plan?"

"They are!" B.J. said.

While Julia and the others were busy glaring at her, Mr. Denton turned to the Corn Flakes. "Do you have this purple notebook they're talking about?" he said.

"Yes," Sophie said.

"Is it a Slam Book?"

"No," Fiona said.

"May I see it?"

Fiona and Kitty both looked at Sophie. Something began to cave in Sophie's chest.

"It's not here at school," she said.

"That's convenient," B.J. said.

Mr. Denton sliced her off with a look.

"Where is it?" he said.

"At my house," Sophie said.

"Well, the sooner you can get it here, the sooner we can get this whole thing straightened out."

"Can't you just trust us?" Fiona said.

"That wouldn't be fair at ALL," Julia said. She looked expectantly at Anne-Stuart.

"That's right," Anne-Stuart said. "If you read ours, then I think you should read theirs."

"Make her call her mom to bring it over here," B.J. said.

Mr. Denton delivered a glare that should have melted B.J. down like candle wax. "I think I can handle this without your help."

"My mom's not home," Sophie said.

"Also convenient," B.J. muttered.

Sophie looked her squarely in the eyes, so hard that Willoughby shrank back against Julia.

"But my father is home," Sophie said. "I'll call him and maybe he'll bring it over."

Sophie could feel Fiona staring at her. Sophie herself couldn't believe she had just said that. But there it was, and she followed Mr. Denton to the office where they let her call her house. "Daddy?" she said when he answered.

"What's wrong, Sophie?" he said. "Are you sick?"

"No—I just need you to bring that purple notebook to me."

"Were you supposed to turn that in or something?" His voice was starting to get brisk.

"Mr. Denton wants to see it," she said.

Mr. Denton held out his hand. "Let me talk to him," he said.

So Sophie gave him the phone and shrank against the counter while Mr. Denton explained the whole thing.

This better be God-space, she thought. *Or I'm doomed.*

Mr. Denton said a few "yes, sirs," and handed the phone back to Sophie.

"Daddy?" she said.

"I'm coming over there, Sophie," Daddy said. She could almost see his jaw muscles going into spasms. "And I am NOT happy."

Twelve

❋ ⬠ ✺

When Sophie's father arrived, Mr. Denton, the Corn Flakes, the Corn Pops, and Maggie were waiting in the conference room in the office.

The minute Sophie saw Daddy, she knew it was all over. His face was purple-red, and his eyes were on fire, and his face was so tight, the muscles couldn't have moved if they'd wanted to.

Before Sophie could even swallow, he spotted her at the table and came straight for her, putting his hands on her shoulders.

Sophie waited to feel his anger sizzling through his fingers. But Daddy's big hands just swallowed her shoulders and stayed there, like pieces of armor.

It didn't occur to her until Mr. Denton said, "Did you bring the notebook, Mr. LaCroix?" that Daddy wasn't carrying anything.

"No, sir, I did not," Daddy said. His voice was too quiet.

"I'd really like to see it—"

"For you to even ask to see it is an extreme invasion of my daughter's privacy, Mr. Denton," Daddy said.

Sophie completely stopped breathing. Fiona stared up at Daddy with her mouth hanging open.

"I was guilty of that myself when I picked it up last night," Daddy went on. "I thought it was a project for school until you called."

"Then it isn't," Mr. Denton said. His face drooped.

"No, it isn't. But it isn't a Slam Book, or whatever you called it, either, I can tell you that." He squeezed Sophie's shoulders. "Do I have your permission to tell him what IS in that book?" he said.

"Yes," Sophie said. She was afraid to say more—in case this was just a dream and she would wake herself up.

"This Slam Book they are suspected of keeping," Daddy said, "is a collection of personal things created by three very creative young women. It is a tribute to the history of our family. There are things in there about my own grandmother that I never knew. It has nothing to do with anyone else here."

Sophie couldn't see Daddy's face, but she could tell he was looking around the table, by the way each Corn Pop was shriveling, one after another.

"If my daughter wants to show the book to you, Mr. Denton, that is her choice. If she decides not to, I will stand behind her."

I will stand behind her.

I will stand behind her.

Suddenly there was so much God-space, it was all Sophie could do not to climb up on the table, arms spread wide, and dance in it.

Instead, she lifted up her chin. "We don't want to turn our notebook over to you, Mr. Denton." She turned to Fiona and Kitty. "Do we?"

"No," Fiona said.

Even Kitty said, "No, we don't."

"But I do want to say something else," Sophie said.

Mr. Denton had a smile playing at the corners of his mouth as he said, "Please do."

Between Fiona and Kitty's questioning looks, Sophie directed her eyes at the Corn Pops. Julia was still trying to maintain the queenly air, but the rest of the hive looked withered.

"I AM seeing a therapist," she said, "but I am NOT mentally underdeveloped and I DON'T have serious problems—even if I AM adopted." She took a deep breath. "Because I know my dad loves me anyway."

"Indeed he does," Mr. Denton said. "Julia, B.J., Willoughby, Anne-Stuart—stay here. The rest of you may go on to class. Mr. LaCroix, you want to talk this out?"

Daddy nodded—sort of absently, Sophie thought—and then he knelt down in front of her.

"I'm picking you up after school," he said. "I think we need to have a talk."

There was no muscle-twitching. Sophie nodded solemnly.

He's going to tell me the truth now, she thought as she left the conference room—with Mr. Denton saying, "Well, Julia and Anne-Stuart, you realize GATE is out of the question for you now." What Daddy was going to say wasn't going to be what she wanted to hear—but it didn't mater now. It really didn't. Because Daddy had just stood up for her.

"Sophie?"

Sophie turned around to see Kitty, hanging next to the water fountain.

"We have to get to class," Sophie said.

"I just wanted to tell you something."

"Okay," Sophie said, "but hurry."

Kitty latched both hands around Sophie's arm. "I have to tell you that all this time I've been staying with you and Fiona and pretending to be a Corn Flake because I didn't want to be by myself. But now I really want to be one." She clung harder to Sophie's arm. "I'm proud to be one."

Sophie could feel her wisp of a smile floating onto her face. They had Kitty now, and it was for real. Now, if only Maggie—

"Oh, I'm supposed to give you this."

Kitty dug her hand into the pocket of her embroidered jeans and pulled out a bright pink piece of paper. For a second it made Sophie shiver, until she opened it and saw the same neat printing that had turned the world upside down.

I WANT TO BE A CORN FLAKE, it said.

Sophie hugged the God-space to her all afternoon. She wasn't even afraid when she climbed into the car with Daddy. Not until he said, "We're going over to Dr. Peter's office." Then she began to sink.

"I thought WE were gonna talk," she said. "You and me."

"We are," Daddy said. "But that's not something you and I do so well, Soph. So I asked Dr. Peter if we could talk over there. He won't be with us—he'll just be around in case we need him."

Dr. Peter showed them both into a small room Sophie hadn't been in before. It had a couple of beanbag chairs, and Daddy folded his big self into one of them, and Sophie curled up in the other.

"I have to say this first," Daddy said. "Sophie Rae, you are not adopted. You are Mama's and my biological kid."

"I AM?" Sophie said. "Are you SURE?"

Daddy's eyebrows went into upside-down V's. "Yes, I'm sure! I was there to see you come into the world. I was the first one to hold you."

Sophie was shaking her head. "Then why aren't there any pictures of me when I was a baby?"

"See, Soph this is the part I never wanted to tell you." He suddenly looked very lost. Sophie was pretty sure she knew the feeling.

He scratched both sides of his head. "Before Mama even got to hold you, the doctors took you off to Neonatal Intensive Care. You were so sick, we didn't think you were going to make it through the first day."

"You thought I was going to DIE?"

"They told us you might. You were born two and a half months before you were supposed to be. You were so small and you had so many things wrong with you—you had to fight for your little life."

Sophie sank back into the beanbag and let that information settle itself into her mind. "We almost lost you four or five times before you were even two years old," Daddy said. "We were so wrapped up in keeping you alive, we didn't even think about taking pictures." He let his head sag for a minute. "I didn't want to take your picture that way. I was afraid that if you lived you would see those photographs and you would always think of yourself as a sick kid. You were a fighter, and THAT's how I wanted you to see yourself."

"When did I get better?" Sophie said.

"Right after you turned two, you seemed to turn a corner. We knew you were going to make it then."

"So that's why I'm underdeveloped," Sophie said.

"The doctors say you'll catch up. Besides, your Mama is just a little bitty thing."

Daddy resituated himself on the beanbag, his long legs sprawled on the floor. "I'm still not clear on how you ever got the idea that you were adopted in the first place."

"I saw that paper."

"What paper?"

"The letter to you and Mama—it said 'Thank you for your interest in adopting a child.'"

"Okay, no more attic for you," Daddy said.

"What did it mean?" Sophie said.

Daddy looked up at the ceiling, as if he were visiting a memory of something he hadn't been to in a long time. "When you were about four and we really knew you were going to be okay, things were going so well for our family that Mama and I decided we wanted to have another kid to share all that with. Only—it didn't happen right away." Daddy shuffled his feet a little. "Anyway, we started looking into adopting and then, bingo, we found out Zeke was on his way."

Sophie's insides were so shaky, she was sure her voice would be too when she said, "So Zeke IS my little brother, and Lacie's my sister, and you and Mama are my parents—"

Daddy said, "We'd be all those things whether you were adopted or not. A family is a family because of love, not because of biology." Daddy leaned toward her. Sophie had never seen his face look confused before, ever. "I got the feeling when I was at the school today that it was the first time you believed I loved you. Is that right?"

Sophie could almost hear Dr. Peter saying, *I love that honesty, Loodle.*

She tangled and untangled her fingers for a few seconds, and then she said, "Yes."

Daddy's face didn't turn red. He didn't demand to know where she got such a ridiculous idea. He just nodded. And he blinked. Hard.

"Look, Soph," he said. His voice was thick, like peanut butter. "The reason I'm so hard on you is because I know God has you here for a very special reason, or you would have died. I want to be sure you have all it takes to fulfill his purpose for you. I want you to be physically strong—that's why I push you toward sports. I want you to get a good education—that's why I'm always raising the bar on your grades. I don't want to see you wasting time on things that don't mean anything."

Sophie shook her head. "I don't do that, Daddy."

To her surprise, he nodded. "I think I'm starting to figure that out, Soph," he said.

And suddenly, Sophie figured something out too. THIS was what it meant when Jesus went home and obeyed his parents and grew up every way he was supposed to. And THEN he did what God put him there to do.

I'm gonna be that obedient too she decided, then and there. *Even when Daddy doesn't get me, I have to respect him.*

And she had to start right now.

"Daddy?" she said.

"Yeah, Soph?" he said.

"Thank you for standing up for me today."

Daddy's big face broke into a grin so wide, Sophie could see right into his God-space.

"You were taking a hit for the team," he said. "I had to be there."

And somehow Sophie knew that he always would be.

Glossary

appalling (uh-PALL-ing) totally shocking or almost heinous

archaeologists (ARE-kay-AH-luh-jists) people who study the stuff that people left behind a long, long time ago

artifact (ARE-tih-fakt) something people used in the past, like tools or artwork

camisole (KAA-mih-sole) a short, sleeveless shirt worn underneath clothes

cardiac arrest (CAR-dee-ack uh-REST) when someone's heart stops beating

clandestine (clan-DEHSS-tin) being secretive and maybe even sneaky

cower (COW-er) to crouch or shield yourself, usually from something scary

descendants (dih-SEHN-dunts) people who are born after a person, like Fiona is Boppa's descendant

despondent (dih-SPAHN-dunt) feeling totally depressed and hopeless

dignity (DIG-nuh-tee) feeling worthy and like you're important; being filled with good pride

documental (DAH-kyou-mehn-tuhl) evidence like an artifact, photograph, or recording that can prove something; usually this evidence has been documented officially in writing

excavate (ECK-skuh-vate) to dig out and remove

flabbergast (FLAA-burr-gaast) to overwhelm with shock or surprise

flux (FLUHKS) the condition of having diarrhea

gavel (GAA-vuhl) a mallet used to gain the audience's attention or confirm a decision was just made; the thing judges use

heinous (HAY-nuhss) shockingly mean, beyond rude, or like wicked in a bad way

jeopardize (JEH-purr-dize) to risk or threaten something dangerously

leeway (LEE-way) freedom given to someone else to make mistakes or do something a different way

mutiny (MYOO-tuh-nee) harshly rebelling against authority, like a sea captain or your parents

obsessed (uhb-SEHST) thinking about something way too much

palisade (paa-luhss-ADE) a fence of stakes used to protect a fort from enemies

precedent (PREH-suh-duhnt) something done or said that serves as a model for someone or something that comes afterward, like a set example to follow

sedately (sih-DATE-lee) quietly and steadily, like in a cool, calm way

swellings (SWELL-ings) puffed up larger than normal size, especially like when it's a body part or area of the body

vexation (veck-SAY-shun) the act of troubling or irritating someone or when you're being troubled or irritated by someone or something

Sophie and Friends

Nancy Rue

Meet Sophie LaCroix, a creative soul with a desire to become a great film director someday, and she definitely has a flair for drama! Her overactive imagination frequently lands her in trouble, but her faith and friends always save the day. This bindup includes two-books-in-one.

Sophie's First Dance: Sophie and her friends, the Corn Flakes, are in a tizzy over the end-of-school dance – especially when invitations start coming – from boys! Will the Flakes break up, or can Sophie direct a happy ending?

Sophie's Stormy Summer: One of the Flakes is struck with cancer, and Sophie severely struggles with the shocking news, until she finds that friends – and faith – show the way to a new adventure called growing up.

Available in stores and online!

Sophie Flakes Out

Nancy Rue

Meet Sophie LaCroix, a creative soul with a desire to become a great film director someday, and she definitely has a flair for drama! Her overactive imagination frequently lands her in trouble, but her faith and friends always save the day. From best-selling author, Nancy Rue, comes two-in-one bindups of the popular Sophie series.

Sophie Flakes Out: Sophie wants more privacy like her friend Willoughby, who has plenty, until Willoughby's father finds out about her fast, new friends. His harsh punishment makes Sophie wonder what rules they need to follow.

Sophie Loves Jimmy: Sophie doesn't get why a rumor should stop her from being Jimmy's friend – until the Corn Flakes start believing the whispers. Now Sophie wonders how she and the Flakes can ever be friends again!

Available in stores and online!

Sophie Steps Up

Nancy Rue

Sophie LaCroix is a creative soul with a desire to become a great film director someday, and she definitely has a flair for drama! Her overactive imagination frequently lands her in trouble, but her faith and friends always save the day. This bindup includes two-books-in-one, Sophie Under Pressure and Sophie Steps Up.

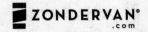

Sophie's Drama

Nancy Rue

Sophie LaCroix is a creative soul with a desire to become a great film director someday, and she definitely has a flair for drama! Her overactive imagination frequently lands her in trouble, but her faith and friends always save the day. This bindup includes two-books-in-one, Sophie's Drama and Sophie Gets Real.

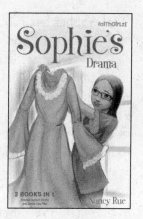

Sophie's Friendship Fiasco

Nancy Rue

Meet Sophie LaCroix, a creative soul with a desire to become a great film director someday, and she definitely has a flair for drama! Her overactive imagination frequently lands her in trouble, but her faith and friends always save the day. From best-selling author, Nancy Rue, comes two-in-one bindups of the popular Sophie series.

Sophie's Friendship Fiasco: Sophie tries living up to other's expectations, but lately she's letting everyone down. When she misrepresents the Flakes – with good intentions – she loses their friendship. Will they ever forgive her?

Sophie and the New Girl: Sophie likes the new girl who joins the film club. She's witty and unique, even if she is a bit bizarre. When the camera goes missing, the other Flakes are quick to accuse. Will Sophie be able to identify the real thief?

Available in stores and online!

NIV Faithgirlz! Backpack Bible, Revised Edition

Small enough to fit into a backpack or bag, this Bible can go anywhere a girl does.

Features include:

- Fun Italian Duo-Tone™ design
- Twelve full-color pages of Faithgirlz fun that helps girls learn the "Beauty of Believing!"
- Words of Christ in red
- Ribbon marker
- Complete text of the bestselling NIV translation

Available in stores and online!

NIV Faithgirlz! Bible, Revised Edition

Nancy Rue

Every girl wants to know she's totally unique and special. This Bible says that with Faithgirlz! sparkle. Through the many in-text features found only in the Faithgirlz! Bible, girls will grow closer to God as they discover the journey of a lifetime.

Features include:

- Book introductions—Read about the who, when, where, and what of each book.

- Dream Girl—Use your imagination to put yourself in the story.

- Bring It On!—Take quizzes to really get to know yourself.

- Is There a Little (Eve, Ruth, Isaiah) in You?—See for yourself what you have in common.

- Words to Live By—Check out these Bible verses that are great for memorizing.

- What Happens Next?—Create a list of events to tell a Bible story in your own words.

- Oh, I Get It!—Find answers to Bible questions you've wondered about.

- The complete NIV translation

- Features written by bestselling author Nancy Rue

Available in stores and online!

ZONDERVAN®
.com

Talk It Up!

Want free books?
First looks at the best new fiction?
Awesome exclusive merchandise?

We want to hear from you!

Give us your opinions on titles, covers, and stories.
Join the Z Street Team.

Email us at zstreetteam@zondervan.com
to sign up today!

Also—Friend us on Facebook!

www.facebook.com/goodteenreads

- Video Trailers
- Connect with your favorite authors
- Sneak peeks at new releases
- Giveaways
- Fun discussions
- And much more!